Janey's Choice

Janey's Choice

Bernice Thurman Hunter

Cover by
Tony Meers

Scholastic Canada Ltd.

Scholastic Canada Ltd.
175 Hillmount Road, Markham, Ontario, Canada L6C 1Z7
Scholastic Inc.
555 Broadway, New York, NY 10012, USA
Scholastic Australia Pty Limited
PO Box 579, Gosford, NSW 2250, Australia
Scholastic New Zealand Limited
Private Bag 94407, Greenmount, Auckland, New Zealand
Scholastic Ltd.
Villiers House, Clarendon Avenue, Leamington Spa,
Warwickshire CV32 5PR, UK

Canadian Cataloguing in Publication Data

Hunter, Bernice Thurman

  Janey's choice

ISBN 0-590-12497-8

I. Title.

PS8565.U577J36 1998   jC813'.54   C98-930948-7

PZ7.H86Ja 1998

5 4 3 2 1   Printed and bound in Canada   8 9 /9 0 1 2 3 4 /0

For Diane, editor and friend.

With grateful thanks to Professor David H. Jenkinson for all his help and encouragement

Contents

Chapter 1

A Breathtaking Question

*J*aney Phair came dashing in the kitchen door, all out of breath. Glancing into the parlour at the closed door of her father's den, she whispered, "Have you asked him yet, Amy?"

"Where on earth have you been?" her sister pointed with a wooden spoon to the moon-faced clock on the wall. The black hands pointed to five-thirty.

"I *told* you I would be late 'cause Miss Jones picked Norma-Jean and me to clean the blackboards."

"Oh, that's right, you did." Amy dipped the spoon into the steaming pot on the stove and began to stir.

"Well . . . did you ask him yet?" persisted Janey as she slipped into her pinafore and began setting the table.

"No. I've decided to wait until after supper."

Janey could hardly bear to wait. She had gotten a letter that morning from her Uncle Wallace in Winnipeg, Manitoba. In it was a breathtaking question which she had to discuss with her father. But her big sister was right. Their dad was always more congenial after he'd eaten.

"Ask him what?" Janey's thirteen-year-old brother Patrick snitched a pickle from the jar and popped it in his mouth.

"Hey, Amy, is my white shirt ironed yet?" Janey's oldest brother, Michael, had just finished pumping water over his head at the kitchen sink. Shaking his curly mop like a dog after its bath, he sent drops of water flying all over the kitchen.

"Mikey! Look what you just did!" scolded Janey as she dabbed at the splattered plates with a dishtowel. But she wasn't really mad at her big brother. Everything he did made her laugh.

"Sorry about that, Shortstop." Mikey winked at her through the looking glass over the sink. Then he combed his hair into shiny black waves and leaned closer to admire himself.

Mikey's handsome, Janey thought. Her second-best friend, Norma-Jean Cox, and her third-best friend, Carol Ann Pocklington, were both crazy about him.

"Ask him what?" Patrick snitched another pickle.

"None of your business, Patty, and keep your fingers out of the pickle jar." Amy nudged him aside and placed a cutting board, piled high with buttered bread, in the middle of the table. "And, no, Mikey, your shirt isn't ironed yet. Who was your servant last year?"

Janey laughed at the old saying. Amy sounds just like Gramma, she thought.

Gramma Davis was dingling her china dinner bell from the parlour, where she sat tucked up under an afghan on the davenport.

"Janey . . . " Amy held out a tray with a bowl of steaming broth and a plate of soda biscuits on it. "Do you think you could to take this in to Gramma without spilling it?"

"I'll try."

Carefully balancing the tray, Janey had one foot on the step between the kitchen and the parlour when her youngest brother, Harry, came running in with his head down and smacked into her elbow. The beef broth slopped over the side of the bowl, washed across the tray, and splashed onto the floor.

"Haar-ry!" shrieked Janey.

Abruptly the door to her father's den flew open and out he came, his bushy black hair standing on end.

"What's going on out here?" he bellowed. "Can't a man get his sleep? It's bad enough working the graveyard shift without being wakened up with all this bellyragging." He ran his fingers through his hair like a comb, rubbed the sleep from his eyes, and frowned down at the floor. "Who made that mess?" he demanded.

"I did, Daddy!" Janey said quickly. Her father always picked on Harry. "I bumped my elbow on the doorjamb."

Instantly his frown changed to a smile. "Clean it up then, Petty," he said giving her head a pat. Harry scowled, but said nothing.

Amy had made their father's favourite supper, beef stew with soda-dumplings, to put him in a good mood. They were all in their places around the oilcloth-covered table when Patty piped up, "Ask him what, Amy?"

Janey kicked him under the table.

"Oww!" Patty yelped. "What did you do that for?"

"Stop talking at the table, all of you," said Amy.

Janey darted her eyes towards her father. The dumpling on his spoon had stopped midway to his mouth. "Ask me what?" he demanded.

"Eat while it's hot, Dad," urged Amy.

"I won't eat a bite." He dropped the dumpling

with a plop back onto his plate. "Not until I hear the question."

It went so quiet around the table that Janey could hear Gramma supping her broth in the parlour. She looked at Amy, and Amy nodded. So she fished Uncle Wallace's letter out of her pinny pocket and handed it to her father.

He read it silently, then tossed it onto the sideboard. "What does he mean by calling himself your 'Papa'? He's not your father. He's not even your blood uncle. He's nothing to you now that your Aunt Bessie's gone."

"Oh, don't say that, Daddy." The mean words stabbed Janey's heart like a knife. "He's not nothing to me. He was my papa for eight years before I came home to you."

He pulled at his chin, and his mouth turned down in a scowl. "Don't you feel at home here, after three years?" he demanded.

"Yes, but . . . "

"But what?"

"But Winnipeg is my home too."

Scraping his chair back from the table her father growled, "Go back there then, if that's what you want." Then he left his favourite supper on his plate and marched through the parlour and out the front door.

Through a blur of tears, Janey stared down at her dumplings, floating like snowballs in a golden pond; she loved Amy's dumplings, so light and fluffy, but she had suddenly lost her appetite.

Chapter 2

The Letter

*T*hat night Janey lay awake in the dark thinking while she waited for her sister to come to bed. When she had first come back from Winnipeg her bed had been made up on the pull-out davenport in the parlour. But her father's loud snoring from the den, had scared her in the night. Sometimes it sounded like a bear in there! So her father had made a room for the boys in the cellar beside the coal bin. It was a ramshackle little room because her father wasn't handy with a hammer and saw. But the boys didn't care — they liked it because nobody could hear them cutting up in the middle of the night.

Then Janey had happily moved upstairs to sleep with Amy, and poor Gramma had unhappily snatched her false-teeth cup off the washstand and her nightshift off the hook on the door and had grumbled her way into the boys' room. She complained bitterly about the boys' bed. She said they had ruined the springs jumping on it and now the thin mattress was all picks and pokes.

Janey had been home in Toronto for three years now. And she was happy with her family. But she always had a funny feeling there was something missing, a feeling she couldn't define.

Her thoughts were interrupted by music floating up the stairwell. No matter how tired she was, Amy always played the piano before she came to bed. The sweet notes of "My Bonnie Lies Over the Ocean" faded softly away and Janey heard the piano lid clack shut. Next she heard Amy's footsteps padding up the stairs into the other room to check on Gramma. At last Amy slipped quietly into their room, shut the door and got undressed in the dark. Janey heard her whisper, "Good night, Mama," to their mother's picture in the ivory frame on the washstand. Amy often talked to the picture, but Janey never did. Their mother had died when she was still a baby, and she couldn't even remember her.

Amy slipped into bed beside her and settled back on the pillow.

"Amy . . . "

"Oh, Janey, you startled me. I thought you were asleep." Amy reached over and patted her hand.

"It's lovely having you for a bedmate, Janey. It was no picnic sleeping with Gramma, I can tell you!"

The thought of sleeping with bony old Gramma made Janey squeal with laughter. Her laugh was contagious and Amy burst out laughing, too.

"You two settle down in there!" squawked Gramma from across the hall. "I need peace and quiet in my old age."

"Sorry, Gramma!" they chorused.

"Amy . . . " whispered Janey, "Can I read you Uncle Wallace's letter again?"

"Yes, but quietly." Amy reached out and switched on the old Tiffany lamp that had been their mother's. It cast a glow over the photo in the ivory frame: a hand-tinted snapshot of a pretty woman with a cloud of chestnut-brown hair, violet eyes and pink smiling lips.

Janey slipped the letter out from under her pillow, propped herself up on the iron bedstead rail and began to read:

> *The Vine Cottage,*
> *110 Elmer Street,*
> *Winnipeg, Manitoba.*
> *June 10, 1931.*

Hello there Chicken . . .

"That's what he always called me because before they got me Aunt Bessie said they had neither chick nor child." Amy smiled and Janey read on.

How would you like to come out for a visit this here summer? Me and Purry-Motor . . .

"Purry-Motor is my cat . . . remember I told you about him? He would have got drowned in a potato-sack with his two sisters if I hadn't rescued him. Then Aunt Bessie let me keep him because she said that saving somebody's life meant they belonged to you forever."

"Go on," whispered Amy, "but lower your voice or we'll hear from Gramma again."

Janey lowered her voice to a murmur.

Me and Purry-Motor have been mighty lonely since your Aunt Bessie went home . . .

Janey had to stop to swallow the lump in her throat.

But Pearl Mead helps me out . . . you remember Pearl, your Aunt Bessie's best friend? Well, she comes in every few days and scolds me for being messy. Then she tidies up the place and cooks me up some grub. She's a good-hearted soul with a core soft as butter, but she's awful bossy. Every word I utter she slaps me with a quote from the Good Book. Like yesterday, I says to her how I miss Bessie more every day and she says to me, "The Lord giveth and the Lord taketh away." And I says to her, *"A fat lot of good that does me,"* and she comes right back with *"Out of the heart the mouth speaketh!"* Ah, but I mustn't complain because the woman does bake a fine apple pie.

Well, Chicken, I hope you're happy there in Toronto with your own folk, and by the way how is that father of yours? And your grandma? I got word from your Aunt Celia, in Orillia, that the old woman is poorly now. You can tell them both I was asking for them.

Now you let me know if your father, there, will send you on the train to Winnipeg. Tell him I'll see that you get back safe and sound. It's been a long time since I've set eyes on you and like I said, it gets mighty lonely.

Lovingly,
Your Papa Wallace

Janey folded the letter and put it back under her pillow. "What are we going to do about Daddy, Amy?" she asked, seeing his scowling face in her mind's eye.

Amy clicked off the lamp and slid under the quilt. "I'll decide tomorrow," she said. "You go to sleep now, Janey, so you' ll be well rested for your final arithmetic exam tomorrow."

"Okey-doke." Janey scratched the tip of her

nose. "But I know enough arithmetic to pass already."

"Don't say okey-doke. Its slang. And I want you to do more than pass. I want you to get honours. You're altogether too happy-go-lucky, Janey Phair."

"But Aunt Bessie always said that the most important thing in life is to be happy," countered Janey.

"Well, you can't be a Pollyanna all your life, you know."

"What's a Pollyanna?"

"A silly girl in a book who was glad all the time and never worried her head about anything."

Janey couldn't help but wish her sister were a little more like that. But she understood why Amy wanted her to excel in school. Amy had had to leave high school without graduating, to help Gramma take care of the family. "And that's not going to happen to you," she had told Janey fiercely. "I promised Mama that I'd watch over all of you, and your education is part and parcel of that promise."

"Okey-doke, Amy. I'll work harder. But what are we going to do about Daddy?"

"Hmmm . . ." Amy murmured. "We'll let sleeping dogs lie for now," she said. "I'm pretty sure he'll come around. You always do seem to get your way with him. Write to Uncle Wallace and say you'll let him know for sure as soon as you can."

The next morning she got up early, wrote Papa Wallace a quick note, stuck on a two-cent stamp, printed SWAK on the back of the envelope, and mailed it on her way to school.

Chapter 3

A Long White Envelope

"What's the matter, Shortstop?" Michael tousled her curly brown hair. "You've been awful quiet lately."

"I'm all right," Janey answered on a big sigh.

"Then close your books and come for supper," Amy said. "I've made Toad-in-the-hole just for you." Toad-in-the-hole was Janey's favourite dish: a crispy brown sausage poking its head like a groundhog out of a mound of mashed potatoes. But today it didn't even tempt her.

Two whole weeks had gone by since the letter had come from 'Papa' Wallace and her father hadn't even mentioned it again. All this time her father had pretended that he didn't even notice that she was picking at her food. But every night at the supper table she could feel him watching her out of the corner of his eye. And to make matters worse, her second-best friend, Norma-Jean Cox, and her third-best friend, Carol Ann Pocklington, had both gone away to High Park Summer Camp so Janey was missing her first-best friend, Esther Pickles back in Winnipeg, more than ever.

This night, their father sat down at the table with a thump and slapped a long white envelope onto her plate. "Now quitcherbellyachin and eat your supper before you shrivel up into a dried old prune like your grandma." He guffawed at his own joke. "And when you're finished, go pack your grip." He turned suddenly to Harry, who gave a nervous little jump. "You, too, young Harry. I don't want your sister going on that long trek all by her own self."

Janey could hardly believe her ears . . . or her eyes, as she pulled two tickets to Winnipeg out of the envelope.

"Oh, Daddy!" She jumped up and threw her arms around his neck so tight he gagged. "Thank you . . . thank you . . . thank you! But . . . "

"But what?"

"But I'd like Amy to go with me instead of Harry."

"Oh, you would, would you? And who, pray tell, would look after things around here? The old woman can't do it any more."

Amy drew in a sharp breath at his words. Both Janey and her father heard it.

"I'm sorry, Amy-girl." Their father's voice was surprisingly gentle. "I'd rather it was you who went along with your sister. You're older and more dependable. But it's not only that you're needed here. It's that I can't afford to send you. Or Mike or Pat for that matter, being as you're seventeen and Michael is fifteen and . . . what's Patrick now . . . thirteen? At any rate you'd all need grown-up fare at twice the price. Only Harold and Jane can travel for children's fare since they're both twelve-and-under. Those are railroad rules, you see."

"I see." Janey heard the disappointment in her sister's voice. Still, Amy managed to smile. "Well, then, they'll both need new rigouts for the trip so I'll want money to take them shopping."

Janey's eyes flashed back to her dad. What might he say about that? she wondered. But he didn't say anything. He just leaned back on the hind legs of his chair, reached into his pants pocket, pulled out a ten-dollar bill and said to Amy, "Here's a sawbuck. That should do it."

ði ði ði

That night Janey stood right by her father's side as he called up Papa Wallace. He dialed O for the operator and she heard the operator's squeaky voice saying, "What number please?" Her father said in a loud voice, "I wish to speak to Mr. Wallace Hogan, Elmer Street, Winnipeg, Manitoba."

He stayed on the line only long enough to tell Uncle Wallace what day and hour she and Harry would arrive in Winnipeg. Then he hung up before Janey even had a chance to speak to her uncle.

"I wanted to say hello," she lamented.

"You can say all the hellos you like when you get there," snapped her father.

Chapter 4

Westward Ho!

*T*wo days later Janey and Harry boarded the Transcontinental train, both decked out in their new rigouts from Eaton's. Harry was wearing "breeks" instead of the long pants he wanted, but Janey was happy with her new pink dress. Their father settled them on the train — Amy had had to stay home because Gramma had suffered a bad spell in the night.

Collaring the conductor in the aisle, John Phair wagged a big finger in the man's startled face. "These here are my children," he barked, "and I'm putting them in your charge. So see that they get safely to Winnipeg or you'll have me to answer to . . . do you read me?"

The conductor backed away from the menacing finger and nervously twisted his waxed moustache. "Yes, sir. Certainly sir. I've taken care of many a child travelling alone and I've never lost one yet."

"Well, don't let this be the first time." Flapping his hand in the trainman's face John Phair waved him away. Then he leaned over his children. "Now you two behave yourselves and don't make any trouble," he growled.

"We won't, Daddy." Janey wished the whistle would blow so her father would have to disembark. And just then it did . . . three sharp warning blasts.

"I'll be off then." He dropped a kiss on Janey's cheek and shook hands with a surprised Harry.

No sooner had he jumped down the iron steps than the conductor clanged them up behind him. He stood on the platform waving — forlornly, Janey thought — as the train steamed out of Toronto's Union Station. Janey and Harry waved back out the window until he was lost from sight.

Excitement bubbled up inside Janey like ginger ale in a glass. She stretched her neck around to see who was on the train. It looked as if she and Harry were the only children on their coach. All the rest of the passengers were grown-ups. One man looked exactly like Santa Claus without the red suit. The lady across the aisle seemed to be travelling alone. She took off her wide straw hat, set it on the empty seat beside her, and patted her blue-grey hair. Then she glanced over at Janey and smiled. Janey smiled back.

Janey had let Harry sit by the window so he could look out.

"Are you happy now, Harry?" she asked. Harry had been acting all grumpy and down-at-the-mouth ever since the trip was planned.

"No, I'm mad," he grumbled.

"Who are you mad at?"

"Our dad."

"Why?

"Because I never wanted to go on this dumb trip in the first place. He just wants to get rid of me. And now I'm going to miss all the summer fun on our street."

"Oh, but you'll have lots of fun on Elmer Street," Janey assured him. Then she noticed that his bottom lip was trembling. "What's the matter, Harry?"

"Nothing!" He sucked in his lip.

Suddenly Janey knew what was the matter with her brother. Harry had never been away from home before. "Don't be scared, Harry," she said, patting his hand. "I'll take care of you. I know all about trains because I came home to Toronto on the train all by myself when I was only eight years old."

Harry jerked his hand away. "I'm not scared and quit telling me that. You've told that old story a hundred times already. And if you know so much about trains then where are we going to sleep to-night?"

"We'll sleep right here." Janey patted the plush wine-coloured seat between them.

"You mean we have to sleep sitting up?"

"No, Harry, the back of the seat goes down and the conductor will bring us pillows and a blanket."

"Well, what if I sleepwalk and fall right off the train?"

"Oh, Harry." He's such a pain, Janey thought. If only Amy could have come instead. "I'll sleep on the outside, so stop fussing. I wasn't afraid to sleep on the seat all the way to Toronto when I was only . . ."

"Don't tell me that again!" snapped Harry.

"Well, stop your whining."

Just then the conductor came swaying down the aisle. "Tickets please! Have your tickets ready."

Spreading his feet for balance, he winked at Janey and Harry. "My, aren't you the handsome couple," he joked. "Honeymooners, are you?"

Janey burst out laughing but Harry turned red as a tomato. "She's my sister," he retorted.

"Well, I beg your thousand pardons," grinned the conductor as he punched their tickets.

When he had passed by, the lady across the aisle leaned over and said, "Since we're going to be neighbours for a few days I think we should introduce ourselves. My name is Mrs. Frost."

"My name is Jane Elizabeth Phair but everybody calls me Janey. And this is my brother, Harold, but we all call him Harry."

"I heard you talking about sleeping together on the seat," said Mrs. Frost. "I've got a reservation in the sleeping car, so your brother can have my seat all to himself. Then he'll be so comfortable he won't feel like sleepwalking."

"Oh, thank you. Did you hear that Harry? Mrs. Frost . . . "

"I heard." Harry interrupted. "Where's the bathroom on this darn train?"

Embarrassed by his rudeness, Janey grabbed him by the hand and pulled him down the aisle.

When they came back, Harry took the window seat again. Mrs. Frost patted the seat beside herself. "Why don't you come over and we'll get acquainted?" she suggested. Janey was only too glad to hop across the aisle.

"It's nice to see you taking such good care of your little brother," remarked Mrs. Frost.

"Oh, Harry's not my little brother. He's twelve and I'm only eleven. He just seems younger than me because he's short for his age and he's spoiled because he's always been the baby of the family."

Harry gave a disgusted grunt and hunched closer to the window.

"But . . . " Mrs. Frost looked puzzled. "How could he be the baby of the family when he's older than you?"

"Well . . . " Janey clasped her hands on her lap. "You see, our mother died when I was only six months old so my Aunt Bessie . . . she was my mother's big sister, like Amy is mine . . . Well, she and Uncle Wallace took me out to Winnipeg to raise me. Then three years ago, when Aunt Bessie died . . . oh, that was sad and awful . . . my Papa Wallace sent me home because he didn't think I would be happy all alone with him. But I would have . . . only he thought I needed my real family. But he's my real family, too. So, you see, I'm all mixed up. It's a terrible dilemma."

Mrs. Frost smiled at the big word. "Did your aunt and uncle adopt you?" she asked.

"Oh, no! Because I wasn't really an orphan, you see."

"I see." Mrs. Frost nodded her head. "Well, look at it this way: aren't you a lucky girl to have two loving families?"

"Yes, I am," Janey agreed. "But it's still a dilemma."

Harry heaved a big sigh from across the aisle.

Glancing over she saw that his shoulders were drooping and his head was pressed against the windowpane. So she said, "I think I'd better go sit with my brother now."

As the afternoon wore on, Harry fell asleep. Janey was too excited to sleep, and Mrs. Frost was playing Solitaire. Janey knew you weren't supposed to interrupt a person playing Solitaire, so she kept quiet and let Mrs. Frost concentrate on her game.

"Harry." She shook her brother awake. "Do you want to play Fish?"

"No," he said, and clamped his eyes shut again.

"Then it's my turn at the window." Reluctantly, Harry wiggled over to the aisle seat and Janey took his place. She wasn't at the window for two minutes when the scenery began to blur and she dozed off.

Chapter 5

Adventures on the Transcontinental

She dreamt that she was home and Gramma was dingling her china dinner bell. Then her eyes popped open and there was the conductor swaying down the aisle ringing a little brass bell. "First call for dinner!" he announced gaily.

Mrs. Frost was on her feet in an instant. "I'm famished," she declared. "You children must be, too. How would you like to come to the dining car with me?"

"Oh, thanks just the same Mrs. Frost, but our big sister packed us enough food for the whole trip." Janey lifted the lid of the wicker basket at her feet. In it was a Thermos bottle full of lemonade, two big packets of peanut-butter and brown-sugar sandwiches, two big squares of cheese, six yellow apples, and a tin full of oatmeal cookies and butter tarts.

"See!" she said.

Mrs. Frost looked at it doubtfully. "I don't think that will last you all the way to Winnipeg," she said.

"Oh, our dad gave us money, too." Janey pulled a beaded change purse — a going-away present from Amy — out of her dress pocket. Snapping it open, she showed Mrs. Frost a blue five-dollar bill.

"Well . . . why don't you save it for later," suggested Mrs. Frost. "I'll be lonely eating all by myself."

"Oh, please, Janey, can we go?" whined Harry.

"Harry's always cranky when he's hungry," Janey explained.

"I am not! Why do you have to tell people that?"

"Oh, all right, Harry. C'mon, then." Harry smiled for the first time since boarding the train.

They followed their new friend through the rolling coaches until they came to the last car before the caboose.

The dining car looked just like a real restaurant. The tables on both sides of the aisle were set with china dishes and cloth napkins and tinkling water glasses. The dinner was roast chicken with sage stuffing and floating island custard for dessert.

As they ate, the green forest and blue skies of Ontario went shimmering past the wide window.

"Isn't this lovely," remarked Mrs. Frost.

"Lovely," agreed Janey, and Harry said, "Swell!"

The first night Janey had trouble sleeping. The second night was even worse. The *clackety-clack* of the steel wheels and Harry's snoring from the other seat kept her wide awake. She got up quietly and crept down the aisle to the tiny bathroom. Sitting on the metal seat, she pinched back the heavy curtains on the narrow window. The night was pitch black. Red cinders from the puffing smokestack went flashing past like fireflies. The whistle sounded eerily as the train rattled over a crossing. Shivering, Janey crept back into her makeshift bed and fell asleep at last. The next thing she knew Harry was tugging at her foot.

"Get up, Janey. I'm hungry," he whined.

They sat quietly in their seats munching on apples and brown-sugar sandwiches for breakfast and staring out at the jagged rocks and giant evergreens. It had been a long, tiresome journey and Harry seemed to be getting grumpier by the mile. Fortunately, though, the train had to make regular stops along the way.

The engine was slowing down now and the conductor came swaying down the aisle, shouting, "Armstrong! Armstrong! Last chance to stretch your legs in Ontario!"

"Why the heck are we stopping here?" grumbled Harry. "This ain't Winnipeg."

"It's called a 'jerkwater' stop, Sonny Boy," the conductor explained. "That means the locomotive has to jerk to a stop to take on coal and water."

Sure enough, the huge steel wheels screeched to a stop and Janey and Harry were first to leap down the iron steps, through a cloud of steam, onto the wooden platform. The hand-painted sign on the red-brick station read: "Welcome to Armstrong. Population 550, more or less."

The station was one long room with a ticket wicket at one end and a lunch counter at the other. On the counter was a plate of sticky buns under a glass lid.

Harry licked his lips. "I'm still hungry, Janey. Have we got any money left?"

She felt in her dress pocket and pulled out a dime. "We can each have one more treat, Harry. Then we'll be broke."

Harry chose a sticky bun and Janey bought herself an all-day sucker.

"I'm gonna stay in here so flies won't land on my bun," Harry said, wriggling onto a waiting-room chair.

"Okey-doke. I'm going outside."

Several other passengers were standing on the

plank platform watching as the trainmen loaded up the coal car and filled the boiler from the water tower. Janey worked her way up to the front. Just then an eastbound freight train went rumbling by with men riding on top. One man, his straggly beard blowing in the wind, waved at her with a red hanky. Janey waved back with her sucker. "What are those men doing up there?" she asked the well-dressed gentleman standing beside her.

"Oh, them." He waved his walking stick at the disappearing freight train. "They're just no-account hobos riding the rods to Toronto."

"Why are they riding the rods to Toronto?"

"Looking for work, most likely."

Janey was about to ask him why he called them no-account hobos if they were looking for work when the conductor appeared at the coach door. "*All-Aboard!*" he shouted above the roar of the engine.

Janey glanced around for Harry but he was nowhere in sight. He must have jumped on board when she wasn't looking. But when she got on the coach she saw that their seat was empty.

Suddenly the warning whistle blasted: *Toot! Toot! Tooooot!* and the train began to move.

"Wait! Wait!" screamed Janey. "Where's Harry?"

The man who looked like Santa Claus leaped to his feet and yanked the emergency cord. The train screeched to a stop and the conductor went sprawling in the aisle.

"Who in blazes pulled that cord?" he yelled as he scrambled to his feet, dusting off the knees of his uniform.

"I did," said Santa Claus. "There's someone missing."

"Who's missing?"

"My brother!" cried Janey, pointing to the empty seat.

"Well, where in blazes did you see him last?"

"In the station on a bench."

"Great balls of fire!" exploded the conductor. He clanged the iron steps down again and galloped into the station. A moment later he returned, hauling a red-faced Harry by the scruff. Lugging him down the aisle, he dropped him into the seat like a sack of potatoes.

"Now you sit right there and don't you move a muscle," he barked. "And you!" he glared at Janey. "You watch him like a hawk. Don't let him out of your sight until we get to Winnipeg. I don't want that father of yours on my backside."

Janey shoved Harry over and sat down beside him. "Where did you go?" she snapped at him.

Everyone in the coach was rubbernecking in their direction. "I went to the bathroom in the station," Harry confessed in a stage whisper. "And the door got stuck. I heard the train whistle so I started hollering my head off. Then the conductor came and kicked the door in."

The coachful of people rocked with laughter. Poor Harry turned beet red again, slumped in his seat and plastered his nose against the window-pane. "I hate this trip," he grumbled, "and I want to go home."

"Well, Harry, never you mind." I'm beginning to sound just like Amy, she thought. "It'll all be worth it when we get there. You'll see."

Harry gave a little grunt and leaned his head on Janey's shoulder. She put her arm around him and he didn't pull away. They fell asleep together.

The next thing they knew the conductor was standing right beside them making a loud an-nouncement. "Ladies and gentlemen . . . and boy and girl . . . " he winked at Janey and Harry to let them know he wasn't mad any more. "Your atten-tion, please! We are now entering the beautiful province of Manitoba."

The words were no sooner out of his mouth than there was a hideous screeching of steel on steel. Lurching and rocking from side to side, the train came to a shuddering, ear-splitting stop.

Janey and Harry were thrown right out of their

seat and their sandwiches went flying. Hat-boxes and bundles sailed through the air from the racks above.

Women screamed and men swore and Janey and Harry sat on the floor, nursing their cracked heads.

Groaning, the conductor hauled himself up from the floor again and staggered down the aisle toward the coach door. Passengers jumped up to follow him but he held up his hand. "Go back to your seats!" he ordered. "This is a railroad emergency." Then he let down the iron steps with a clang and jumped out onto the cinder path beside the tracks.

Everybody in the coach started cranking their windows open to look outside.

"Open our window, Harry," cried Janey. They both leaned out to see what was happening. Spread out before them, like a sea of gold, was a shining field of wheat. A red brick farmhouse and a tall white silo were silhouetted on the blue horizon.

"Where did all the rocks and trees go?" asked Harry.

"We're on the prairies now. Isn't it beautiful?" But before he could answer the conductor reappeared, his braided cap on crooked and his waxed moustache all askew. Straightening his cap and twisting his moustache back into spikes he hollered, "May I have your attention please!" Obediently, the coach went perfectly silent. Then he announced importantly, "It seems we have had the misfortune to hit a cow."

Janey screamed, "Oh, no!" and clapped her hand over her mouth.

"Did we kill it?" asked Mrs. Frost.

"Don't know," replied the conductor. "I'm waiting for word from the engineer."

Then Harry, who was still hanging out the window, yelled, "There it is! I see it running through the field."

Stretching her neck past Harry, Janey caught a glimpse of the cow's head bobbing in the sea of wheat. Then she saw a little man running after it, waving a straw hat in the air. "Here comes the farmer!" she cried.

Suddenly, without a warning whistle, the train gave a giant lurch forward.

"Close the windows before the coach is full of cinders!" shouted the conductor.

As Janey and Harry cranked their window shut they saw the farmer standing stock-still, shaking his fist at the train. The Transcontinental was moving at a steady clip, now, under a full head of steam, and the farmer soon disappeared from sight.

The coach was buzzing like a beehive. Everybody was talking at once.

"That'll give you something to write home about, Janey," Harry said.

"Oh, that's a good idea, Harry, thank you." Janey got her copybook from her grip under the seat. "Let me sit by the window, so I can see to write."

She had filled two pages when Harry said, "I saw the cow limping, Janey. Do you think that means he'll have to be put down?"

Janey shook her head at his ignorance. "Cow's aren't he's, Harry, they're she's. Anyway, I don't think so . . . the cowcatcher probably saved her."

"What's a cowcatcher?"

"It's the big bumper in front of the engine. I'll show it to you next time we stop. Now be quiet, Harry, so I can think." Licking the tip of her pencil, she continued to scribble.

Mrs. Frost looked over curiously from across the aisle. "What is your sister writing?" she asked Harry.

"Oh, just another story. Janey makes everything that happens into a story."

"Well, then, we'll have to be quiet so she can concentrate," said Mrs. Frost. She opened her book and began to read.

Harry stared out the window until Janey looked up from her copybook. "I remember once when Purry-Motor got kicked by the bread man's horse," she reminisced. "He was hurt so bad that I was sure he was going to have to be put down, but Aunt Bessie made splints out of little sticks for his broken legs and I fed him warm milk with an eyedropper and in about two weeks he was as good as new. So I think the cow will be all right, Harry."

"I think so, too," agreed Mrs. Frost. She had her compact out of her purse and was dusting her nose with face-powder.

Closing her copybook, Janey got her comb and mirror out and tugged at her tangled brown curls. Then she stared at herself in the glass. I wonder if Papa Wallace will recognize me? she thought. Three years is a long time. I hope Purry-Motor hasn't forgotten me. I can hardly wait to see him again.

Harry must have read her mind. "Hey, Janey, how come you named your cat Purry-Motor? That's a dumb name for a cat."

Janey laughed and her blue eyes sparkled. "Wait'll you hear him, Harry. Then you'll know. Papa Wallace always says he sounds like a motor-car without a muffler."

Chapter 6

The Gateway
to the West

"*N*ext stop, Winnipeg! Winnipeg, Manitoba, the gateway to the West!" announced the conductor.

Janey felt a rush of joy that took her breath away.

"Come along, you two honeymooners." The conductor winked at them. "I'll get your grips. You go stand at the gate so you'll be the first ones off. And be sure to give my regards to that uncle of yours. Give him my sympathy, too. Har! Har! Har!"

Janey was so excited that she almost forgot to say goodbye to Mrs. Frost. But the kind lady caught her hand and said, "I hope you have a happy holiday, dear, and that you solve your big dilemma."

"Thank you. Goodbye, Mrs. Frost. Say goodbye, Harry."

As the train rumbled into Winnipeg's Union

Station Janey peered anxiously through the cloud of steam at the upturned faces on the platform.

Suddenly one face stood out from all the others. It belonged to a short man wearing a white Panama hat and a bow tie with flashing lights.

"Papa! Papa!" she screamed. But her voice was drowned out by the din of the puffing steam engine. "There he is, Harry!"

"Where? Which one?"

"The one with the flashing bow tie."

"That's weird," Harry said.

"Oh, no. That's his Celebration Tie," Janey explained. "He only wears it for special occasions. *Papa! Papa! Papa!*"

He spotted her then and his face lit up. The minute the iron steps were down Janey leapt to the platform and ran straight into his arms.

"Whooee!" he cried, swinging her off her feet. Then he set her down and held her at arm's length. "You've grown like a weed, Chickie. And you're pretty as a picture. If only your Aunt Bessie could see you now."

"Oh, Papa!"

Taking her by the shoulders he turned her gently around. "And who might this big fella be?" he asked.

Harry was standing back awkwardly, holding onto the grips.

"That's our Harry, Papa. Don't you recognize him?"

"Can't say as I do." Wallace Hogan leaned forward to shake Harry's hand. "Last time I saw you, Nipper, you were no bigger than a tadpole."

"How do you make them lights work?" Harry was fascinated by the Celebration Tie.

Wallace Hogan chuckled and patted his breast pocket. "Battery," he said. Then he took the grips from Harry's hands and cried, "Follow me, Chickens!" He led the way like a mother hen through the long corridor, under the station's high domed ceiling, and out onto Main Street.

"Oh, look, Harry!" Janey pointed across the street to a majestic stone building. "That's the Fort Garry Hotel. Aunt Bessie said the Prince of Wales slept there once. Didn't he, Papa Wallace?"

"If your Aunt Bessie said so," grinned her uncle.

Harry just grunted.

The same old tin lizzie that Janey remembered was parked at the curb. Uncle Wallace strapped their grips to the running board and they all hopped in.

"We'll take the sightseeing route," said Uncle Wallace, "so your brother, here, can get acquainted with Winnipeg."

Gazing out the window, Janey felt the years rolling backwards like the tide. Everything looked so familiar.

Uncle Wallace made a left turn at the wide, windswept corner of Main Street and Portage Avenue. A sheet of newspaper, like a capricious kite, went sailing past the windscreen. It reminded Janey of another windy day when she and Aunt Bessie had been standing on that very corner waiting for the lights to change: a gust of wind had blown Aunt Bessie's hat right off and it had got caught up on a telephone pole. Her hairpins flying loose in the wind, Aunt Bessie had laughed. "I didn't like the silly old thing anyway. C'mon, Sweetie-pie, you and me are going to Eaton's to get ourselves new bonnets." Janey sighed, remembering.

Uncle Wallace drove slowly through the city's wide avenues until he came to the corner of Osborne Street and Broadway. Then he circled around a magnificent limestone edifice surrounded by trees and gardens. "That's our Legislative Building, Henry. It's like Toronto's Queen's Park, but I think it's even finer, if I do say so myself."

Uncle Wallace stopped the car and pointed out the window. "Take a gander up there," he said.

Craning their necks, Harry and Janey stared up to the very top. There, on the crest of a huge green dome, glittering like gold in the afternoon sun, was the gilded statue of a running boy. In his right hand he held a torch aloft and in the crook of his left arm he carried a sheaf of wheat.

"Who's that supposed to be?" Harry asked.

"He's the spirit of youth," Uncle Wallace explained.

"He's our Golden Boy, Harry. Isn't he beautiful?"

Harry just grunted. Then he looked out the opposite window and asked, "What's that water out there?"

"I think it's the Assiniboine River," Janey said.

"That's right, Chicken. And if you follow it downstream about half a mile it joins the Red River at the Forks. How would you like to go fishin' at the Forks one day, Nipper?"

Instead of grunting, Harry cried, "Swell!"

Then Janey said, "Can we go home now, Papa?"

Smiling down at her anxious face he said, "You bet your boots, Chickie. Hang on to your hats!" Jamming the car into gear, he tramped down on the accelerator and off they flew at twenty-five miles an hour.

Chapter 7

The Vine Cottage

*L*eaving the big city behind, the tin lizzie rattled its way to Winnipeg's western outskirts and came to a shuddering stop in a cloud of dust in front of number 10 Elmer Street.

The instant the car stopped shaking, Janey jumped out and flung open her arms. "Hello the house!" she cried. "It's me, Janey Phair. I'm home!"

The Vine Cottage was a four-room house covered in crimson ivy. It had a pointed roof, a small door, a square window and three cement steps that sat right on the sidewalk because there was no front lawn.

Standing beside his sister, Harry said, "Why do you call this funny little house 'home,' Janey? Our home is the purple house in Toronto."

Janey shrugged her shoulders. "Well, then, I guess I've got two homes, Harry. The Vine Cottage is still my home, isn't it, Papa?"

Her uncle patted her shoulder. "As long as I'm topside, Chickie," he said with a catch in his voice.

Just then the door swung open and out stepped a plump woman with frizzy, salt-and-pepper hair, wearing a printed housedress.

"Well, the Lord be praised!" she cried, and held out her two fat arms. "If it isn't the prodigal chicken come home to roost."

"Pearl!" Janey bounded up the steps into the arms of her Aunt Bessie's best friend. Then, with her heart in her mouth, she squeezed past Pearl and walked slowly down the hall.

The house still smelled like Aunt Bessie: a combination of lavender and lemon oil and frying onions and fresh-baked bread. Janey stopped at the kitchen door and stared in amazement. In three years nothing had changed: the little kitchen was still crowded with homemade furniture. Egg cups full of violets sat on the window ledge as if Aunt Bessie had just put them there. Besides the hall door, where Janey stood, three more doors led off the kitchen to the sitting room and bedchambers.

Suddenly, like a bolt from the blue, an orange ball of fluff leapt from the top of the kitchen cabinet and landed on her shoulder.

"Purry-Motor!" she cried and buried her face in

his fur. Bunting his head under her chin, he began a loud, rumbling purr.

"Now I know why you named him that," Harry said. "He *does* sound like a motor-car without a muffler."

Pearl had the table all set for afternoon tea. "I thought you might fancy a bite after your long journey," she said. "So sit yourselves down. I hope Lazy Daisy cake is still your favourite, Janey Phair."

"Oh, Pearl, you remembered." Janey was so touched she nearly cried. Pearl pinched her cheek and cut the cake into big thick squares, the brown-sugar topping cracking like glass.

Harry managed to stuff down three squares. Then he gulped his milk and said, "Hey, Uncle Wallace. Did you notice our train was late?"

"I sure did." Wallace Hogan pushed back his chair from the table and lit up his pipe.

Pearl pouched her lips disapprovingly. "If the Lord had intended folks to smoke, Wallace," she scolded, "he would have put chimneys on their heads."

Janey and Harry burst out laughing, but their uncle acted like he didn't hear a thing.

"Its not like the Transcontinental to be late," he said, sending a cloud of smoke to the ceiling. "What in tarnation happened?"

"We hit a cow!" cried Janey.

"Aww! Let me tell it," whined Harry. "You tell everything."

"Oh, go ahead and tell it then," she said, wishing once again that Amy had come instead.

While they chatted, Pearl Mead did the washing up. Then she put on her straw bonnet and tied it under her chins. "I'll leave you folks to catch up with your news," she said as she made her way to the door.

"Hold on to your horses, woman." Wallace Hogan tipped back on his chair, fished a crumpled bill out of his pants pocket, and handed it to her. "Here's something for your trouble."

"Well, now, that's mighty generous of you, Wallace." Pearl folded the bill and dropped it in her satchel. "The Lord loveth a cheerful giver."

Janey giggled as the door shut behind Pearl. "She hasn't changed a bit since I was a little girl," she said.

"Some things never change," Uncle Wallace agreed as he tamped out the fire in his pipe with his thumb and put it in his vest pocket. "Like the fact that I have to go back to the shop this afternoon to finish up a job of work." He had put away his Celebration Tie and had changed into his work clothes.

"Can we come with you, Papa?" asked Janey.

"Not this time, Chickie. This job wouldn't be to

your liking. You take your brother up the street and introduce him to your gang."

As soon as Uncle Wallace went out the door Harry said, "What did he mean, about you not liking his job of work?"

"Well . . . you know Uncle Wallace is a furniture maker."

"Yeah. Amy told me."

"Well, he doesn't just make furniture, Harry. He makes coffins, too. That's why his shop is called Hogan's Fine Furniture and Coffin Shop."

Harry shuddered. "I'd be scared of coffins," he said.

"Well, never mind, Harry. Let's go find my friends."

"Maybe they won't like me." Harry hesitated at the door.

"They'll like you because you're my brother. I've got lots of friends here, Harry. Especially the Pickles twins, Esther and Edward. Esther is my very best friend. The night before I left for Toronto, three years ago, we swore an oath that we would be best friends forever."

"I thought Norma-Jean Cox was your best friend," Harry said.

"No. Norma-Jean is my second-best friend. Esther Pickles will always be my first-best friend. C'mon, Harry." She grabbed his hand and ran him up the street.

Chapter 8

Janey's Gang

*E*very house they passed brought back a rush of memories. How many times, Janey wondered, had she and Aunt Bessie strolled up this very sidewalk together?

At the far end of the street, through the massive elm trees, she could see the red brick schoolhouse.

Elmer Street School. Her old school!

Dropping Harry's hand, she raced the rest of the way and stopped for breath at the gate of the chain-link fence. A gang of kids was yelling and chasing each other in a game of touch-tag. Suddenly one girl stopped dead, as if she was playing statues, and stared across the schoolyard.

"Janey? Janey!"

"Essie! Essie!"

Squealing with glee, they flew into each other's arms. Then the rest of the gang was milling around them. Janey was the centre of attention. Everybody bombarded her with questions: "Have you come home to stay, Janey?" "Don't you like Toronto no more?" "Winnipeg's nicer ain't it?" Then a girl Janey didn't recognize piped up, "My mother says that Toronto is full of stuck-ups."

Janey stared into the glittery green eyes of a pretty girl with strawberry-blonde curls. "Who are you?" she asked.

Then Esther Pickles said, "Oh, I'm sorry, Janey. I didn't introduce you. This is Irma Pringle. Her family moved here from Saskatoon, Saskatchewan, last year. She's my best friend."

Essie's best friend? Then who am I? Janey wondered.

Just then Harry started pulling at her sleeve and begged in his whiniest voice, "C'mon, Janey. Let's go home. I'm tired of standing here."

Ignoring Irma Pringle as best she could, Janey said, "I have to go now, Essie. I'll be seeing you." She turned on her heel and walked quickly away with Harry.

"I'll call for you tomorrow, Janey!" Essie called after her, but Janey didn't look back.

That night they sat around the kitchen table with Uncle Wallace, finishing up the Lazy Daisy cake.

Sipping his coffee, Uncle Wallace said, "So tell

me, Janey, how are things back in Hogtown?"

Janey told him all about Amy and Gramma and how the boys were doing at school.

"And your father . . . is he still employed at Lever Brothers?"

"Yes, Daddy's a foreman at the soapworks now," she boasted. "And every payday he brings home boxes of Lux Flakes and Rinso, so we never have to buy soap chips at the store."

"That's mighty handy," agreed her uncle.

Suddenly Harry's head hit the table and he started to snore.

Uncle Wallace laughed. "C'mon, Chickie," he said to Janey. "Let's make up the daybed for your brother. It's been a long day for the both of you."

The daybed in the sitting room was covered with a patchwork quilt that Aunt Bessie had made. Every patch was a memory for Janey: a square of Papa's checkered shirt, a round sunflower from Aunt Bessie's housedress, a diamond-shaped piece from her own polka-dot pinafore. Janey stroked her hand lovingly over the quilt.

They let Harry sleep until his bed was ready. Then Janey shook him by the shoulders. "C'mon, Harry, it's time for bed," she said, leading him like a sleepwalker into the sitting room. "I've laid out your nightshirt so when you're all ready Papa Wallace and I will come back and tuck you in."

Harry looked warily at the daybed. Then he leaned down, lifted up the edge of the quilt and peered nervously underneath. "Hey, what's this under here?" he cried, pulling on an iron ring attached to the floor.

"Oh, that's just the trapdoor to the fruit cellar," Uncle Wallace explained. "It's strong as steel. It won't let you down."

"A trapdoor! I ain't sleeping over no trapdoor!"

"Oh, Harry, don't be such a baby. There's nothing down there to hurt you. Now get into bed or I'll write and tell Daddy what a bad boy you are." She loved Harry, but sometimes she wished he wasn't such a scaredy-cat.

The threat worked and at last Harry was tucked in.

"I think I'll go to bed now, too, Papa," Janey said on a great big yawn.

"Run along then, Chickie, and have a good night's rest." He bent down and kissed her forehead. "I'm mighty happy you're home, girl. It'll be worth getting up in the morning."

"I'm happy, too, Papa. Goodnight."

Her bedroom hadn't changed one bit either. The furniture Papa Wallace had made her — the bird's eye maple bedstead and the dresser with the heart-shaped mirror — looked as if it had never been touched. Above her bed hung a picture, in a criss-cross frame, of two young girls in old-fashioned dresses, their arms around each other, their heads tilted sideways to show off their kiss-curls. The two girls were Aunt Bessie and Janey's mother, Lavinia. "My mother does look just like me," Janey thought with a smile.

She undressed quickly and climbed into bed with Purry-Motor. The bed was sweet and cosy. She wondered if Amy liked being alone in the double bed. Or had Gramma crawled back in beside her? Poor Gramma . . . how she hated the boys' bed.

"It's nice having a bed all to myself," she thought. Then she snuggled down with the marma-lade cat in her arms and kissed between his ears. "But I'm glad I've got you, Purry-Motor."

The cat patted her face with his cushiony paws. Then he started up his motor and his rumbling rhythm soon lulled her off to sleep.

Chapter 9

Nightmare!

A piercing cry in the middle of the night sent Purry-Motor yowling to the ceiling.

Leaping out of bed, her heart clattering, Janey collided with Uncle Wallace in the kitchen. Another scream ripped the air and they bumped into each other trying to get through the sitting-room door.

Uncle Wallace switched on the ceiling light and there was Harry, wild-eyed, standing on the daybed with his back pressed to the wall.

Recognizing the familiar terror in her brother's eyes, Janey jumped up on the bed and hugged him around the waist. "Wake up, Harry!" she cried. "It's just a nightmare!"

"Get away from me!" he yelled, giving her a sudden push that sent her crashing to the floor. Then Uncle Wallace grabbed him in a bear hug. Harry's feet beat the air, and he screamed, "Get it away from me! Get it away from me!"

Hanging on tight, Uncle Wallace sat down on the bed and cradled Harry in his lap. "You're all right now, lad. You're safe and sound with Janey and me."

Janey got up from the floor rubbing her scraped elbows. "What's the matter, Harry? Did you have a bad dream?" she asked.

"He's not a dream. He's real, and he's under there." Harry drew up his feet and pointed under the daybed.

"Who's under there?" asked Uncle Wallace.

"The monster," answered Harry in a frightened whisper. "He pushed up the trapdoor with his humpback and squashed me against the wall."

"Where is he now, Harry?" Janey knew it was only a dream, but it made her blood run cold just the same.

"He's gone back down," Harry whispered.

"Well, if he's down there . . . " Uncle Wallace set Harry on his feet. "We'll flush him out." He went into the kitchen and came back with a flashlight.

Pulling the bed away from the wall, he took hold of the iron ring and scraped open the trapdoor. Out puffed a cloud of damp, musty air. Dropping to his knees, he shone the torch down into the dark dugout. "Come over here, Sport," he said.

"No!" Harry hid behind Janey. "I'm scared."

"Well, you'll be scared of your own shadow for the rest of your born life if you don't come and see for yourself," insisted Uncle Wallace. But Harry didn't budge.

Janey was just about to say, "Don't be such a sissy, Harry," when she remembered the day that Harry had saved Norma-Jean's little brother, Lester-de-pester, from being trampled to death by the Canada Bread man's runaway horse. Norma's father had called Harry a hero that day.

She turned to him and said, "Harry. You weren't scared of a runaway horse on Wheeler Street. So why would you be scared of an imaginary monster?"

Harry looked surprised. Then he put on a brave smile, walked across the carpet, and knelt down beside his uncle.

Uncle Wallace played the light all around the hole and down the slimy ladder.

Taking the torch from his uncle's hand, Harry drew in his breath and said, "You coming, Jancy?" Then he turned around and started down the ladder. Janey followed him reluctantly. She didn't really like the fruit cellar; it was damp and cobwebby and cold, but she knew her brother needed her.

The walls were lined with shelves that held jars and jars of preserves. Each jar was labelled: citron, sand cherries, rhubarb, saskatoons, blueberries, carrots, beans, peas. Picking up a jar, Janey wiped a cobweb off and her heart went *thump* as she recognized Aunt Bessie's handwriting: "Blueberries, picked and done down by Bessie Hogan and Janey Phair, July 23, 1928."

Harry read the label over her shoulder. "Them berries are three years old. They'll be rotten," he said.

"No, they won't, Harry. We'll take them up and have them for supper tomorrow."

"Well, did you find the monster, Sport?" Uncle Wallace was peering down at them. Suddenly Harry swung the spotlight right up under his uncle's nose. "Yeah! There he is!" he laughed.

Uncle Wallace gave them a hand up and lowered the trapdoor. Then Harry helped him lift the daybed back into place.

Janey fixed the covers and plumped up the pillow. "Harry, if you like I'll sleep here tonight and you can have my room," she said.

"*No!*" Harry jumped into bed and pulled the covers up under his chin. "This here is *my* bed."

"Good lad!" declared Uncle Wallace.

From that moment on, Janey saw a big change in Harry. It was as if he had grown up overnight.

Chapter 10

Celebrity

*T*he next morning they were eating breakfast late, still in their nightclothes, when Pearl Mead came bustling in the kitchen door. "Laziness is next to sinfulness," she scolded, handing Uncle Wallace last night's paper. "Back page," she said as she tied on her apron and got the broom from the corner. "Cleanliness is next to godliness," she added, setting right to work.

Janey giggled and Uncle Wallace rolled his eyes. Then he turned to the back page of the local newspaper. As he read, a big grin spread across his face. He folded the paper in half and placed it in front of Janey, pointing to the gossip column: "What's New In Town" by Miss Elsie Mead, who just happened to be Pearl's daughter.

Janey read out loud:

Miss Jane Elizabeth Phair and her brother, Master Harold Phair, hailing from Toronto,

*Ontario, have arrived in town. Miss Jane
was raised in Winnipeg but had the misfortune, through no fault of her own, to be born
in Hogtown and her brother suffered the
same fate. Be that as it may, the two children
are now the happy visitors of their uncle, Mr.
Wallace Hogan of Elmer Street. Mr. Hogan is
a native Winnipeger and proprietor of
Hogan's Fine Furniture and Coffin Shop. He
is also known around town for his unique
Celebration Tie. This columnist wishes Miss
Jane and Master Harold an enjoyable stay in
our fair city.*

"Holy moly!" cried Harry. "We're famous!"

"Can I cut it out and send it home to Amy, Papa?"
asked Janey.

"Go ahead, Chicken. I'm pretty sure Pearl, here,
can get us a few extra copies."

"Pride cometh before a fall," sniffed Pearl as she
dropped a pile of papers at his elbow.

Right after breakfast Janey wrote a long letter
to her sister, and shorter ones to Norma-Jean and
Carol Ann. She told them all about the train trip
and Harry's nightmare and she sent them all a copy
of Elsie Mead's gossip column.

ಶೇ   ಶೇ   ಶೇ

The Vine Cottage,
Winnipeg, Manitoba,
July 13, 1931.

Dearest Amy:

You didn't answer my first letter with the newspaper clipping in it. I guess Gramma is still sick and you are busy.

We have been here for two weeks now. At first it was fun and exciting. Mrs. Pickles (the twins' mother) gave us a welcome party with balloons and a cake with a sparkler on it left over from Firecracker Day. All the kids in the neighborhood came and we played parlour games and musical chairs. Mrs. Pickles played the piano but she does not play beautiful like you, Amy. She makes lots of mistakes and says "drat!" and starts all over again.

Papa Wallace and Mr. Pickles took Harry and Eddie (Esther's twin) fishing in the river and Pearl Mead took me to the show. We saw Min and Bill *starring Marie Dressler (Pearl says she is a Canadian lady, born in Ontario) and Wallace Beery. Pearl invited Essie to go with us but she said she had to go downtown shopping with her mother. Then I found out later that she didn't go downtown at all. She really went to her new friend Irma Pringle's house. I don't like Irma Pringle. Every time the three of us are together she says in a singsong-y voice, "Two's company . . . three's a crowd." And the worst part is, Essie giggles as if she likes it. Also, Irma always says to me, "Oh, Janey, why don't you get your hair cut? Long curls aren't in style any more." Then she shakes her short strawberry curls in my face. So I've decided never to cut my hair.*

The best part of our visit so far is that I have never seen Harry so happy. He and Papa Wallace get on like a house afire. They play dominoes nearly every night. I don't like dominoes so I write stories instead. I finished the story I started on the train and I wrote a ten-page story about Purry-Motor and his girlfriend, Primrose, who lives next door.

Harry often goes to work with Papa Wallace. He loves woodworking and Papa let him sandpaper a coffin lid. Papa says there's one good thing about his job: even in hard times folks can't help dying so he'll always be in work. Only he doesn't say dying, he says cashing in their chips, or kicking the bucket. That makes it sound more like fun.

Harry and Eddie Pickles hit it off right away. Harry says they are best buddies. Like Essie and me used to be before Irma Pringle stuck her nose in!

On Sunday you'll never guess where Papa Wallace took us. To Greenlawn Cemetery! We left the lizzie at the side of the road and walked in. Harry ran across graves and Papa scolded him and told him to skirt around the graves out of respect for the people underneath.

Then we came to a grave that looked like a big pillow of flowers. There was a pink marble stone at the head of the flower bed and Papa whispered to me, "Read the words, Chickie." So I did and this is what it said: "Hogan, Elizabeth Jane 'Bessie' Davis, beloved wife of Wallace Hogan, dear aunt of Jane Elizabeth Phair. 1875-1928. Rest In Peace."

Seeing my own name carved on a gravestone gave me a turn, as Gramma would say. But I knew it was Papa Wallace's way of showing me how much he and Aunt Bessie loved me.

Amy . . . why don't we ever visit our mother's grave? Where is it, do you know?

Does it have a stone with her name on it? Will you take me there someday?

I'll sign off now, Amy, so please write soon. Give my love to Gramma and Daddy and Mikey and Patty.

Your loving sister,
Janey Phair

A few days later a letter finally arrived from Amy.

The Purple House,
July 17, 1931.

Dear Janey:

I am sorry I have not written sooner. I am so busy taking care of Gramma that I hardly have time to clean the house and do the washing. The boys are not much help and Father is out all the time. He works the day shift now and I'm worried he might be drinking again. I asked him last night where he was going and he said "That's for me to know and you to find out!" (How foolish!) Well, by the time he comes home I am in bed (I'm even too tired to play the piano before bed, but I'm glad you think I play better than Mrs. Pickles) so I can't tell what condition he's in. I am essentially the mother in this house now that Gramma is too ill to be in charge.

Janey looked up the word "essentially" in Uncle Wallace's dictionary: *"essential: necessary, indispensable."* The word described Amy to a T.

Gramma is dingling her bell again so I'll have to go now. Janey. Father and the boys will soon be home for supper and I haven't got the potatoes peeled yet.

You and Harry stay out there with Uncle Wallace as long as you like. Don't hurry home. Give them both my love.

P.S. You asked about our mother's grave. It is in Mount Pleasant Cemetery here in Toronto. No, there is no stone on it. That's why I don't go there. It makes me too sad.

Janey turned the page over. It was empty. Amy had forgotten to sign her name.

Chapter 11

A Bad Omen

Janey was just finishing up the lunch dishes when Esther and Irma peered through the screen door. "Come on in!" she called to them.

Esther had invited Janey to go to the picture show with her and Irma. "I wish Essie and me could go alone," Janey thought. But she decided not to say anything.

Just as Esther pushed open the door, a little brown sparrow flew past her into the house.

"*Eeek!*" screeched Irma, running to a corner and flinging her skirt up over her head.

Squeaking and diving with fright, the poor little bird landed with a jerk on the curtain rod.

Irma peeked over the hem of her dress and let out another "*Eeek!*" that scared the sparrow right out of the kitchen and sent it swooping through the door into the sitting room. They heard a clunk, and then silence. Irma looked as if she was going to scream again so Janey hissed, "Shhh!" as she crept to the sitting-room door.

The little bird had hit the window. He was wobbling on the sill, blinking his beady eyes and fluttering his downy wings.

Just then Pearl bustled into the kitchen carrying a grocery bag. She dropped the bag on the table and yanked Irma's skirt down. "For mercy sakes, girl, cover your drawers," she snapped. "Modesty is a virtue." Then she saw Janey in the doorway. "What is it, Janey? What's the matter?"

"Shhh," Janey pressed her finger to her lips. "There's a scared little baby bird in the sitting room. He came in with Essie and . . . her."

"Oh, my soul . . . " Pearl's hand flew to her throat. "That's a bad, bad omen."

"Can you help me catch him, Pearl? He's scared from all that eeking." She darted Irma a disdainful glance.

"You hold open the kitchen door, Janey, and I'll try to guide him out."

Pearl was flushed from the chase by the time the terrified little creature found the door and made his break for freedom.

"It's safe to look now, Irma." Janey couldn't resist the sarcasm.

Smoothing her dress, Irma said, "Let's go, Essie. I don't like this house."

Esther put her arm around Irma as they left and Janey heard her whisper, "There, there, don't be scared," as if she were a baby.

Disgusted, Janey decided not to follow them. Pearl was sitting at the table fanning her face with her apron. Janey sat down beside her and propped her chin in her hands. "Pearl," she said. "What did you mean about the bird being a bad omen?"

Pearl got up and began unloading the grocery bag. "Never you mind, it's nothing. Away you go with your friends."

But Janey didn't budge. "I'm not going anywhere until you tell me," she said.

Putting the can goods away in the kitchen cabinet, Pearl said, "I guess you might as well know." Her voice dropped mysteriously. "A bird in the house portends a death in the family."

The same shivery feeling that she'd felt when she saw her name on Aunt Bessie's gravestone went creeping up Janey's spine. "Is that just an old wives' tale?" she asked hopefully. "That's what my gramma calls old sayings like that."

"Some folks think so." Pearl dumped the bag of flour into the tin bin in the cabinet. "But my mother believed it."

Just then Esther reappeared at the screen door. "Are you coming or not, Janey?" she asked impatiently. "You're making us late."

"You two go without me," Janey said.

"Well, suit yourself," sniffed Essie. She sounds just like Irma, Janey thought.

From his favourite perch on top of the cabinet Purry-Motor leaped gracefully onto Janey's shoulder. Wrapping himself around her neck like a fur collar, he licked her ear with his scratchy tongue and mewed softly.

"I think he's trying to tell you something," said Pearl.

Janey sighed and scratched Purry's nose. "I really miss Norma-Jean," she told Pearl. "She's my best friend back home. I always called her my second-best friend because I thought Essie Pickles was my first, but I'm not so sure any more. Norma and I have lots of fun together, except when she has to mind her little brother, Lester-de-pester."

"Mercy, what a terrible name for a child," said Pearl, poking her head through the hole in her apron and tying the strings behind her back.

"Oh, his name is just Lester but we call him De-pester because he's such a pest. Every time he comes to the purple house he gets in trouble and Gramma sends him home."

"Why on earth do you call your Toronto home the purple house, Janey? It's such a queer name."

"Because it really is purple, Pearl. I'll tell you what Amy told me: When my mother and father got married they moved into our clapboard house on Wheeler Street. It was painted grey, then, and Mama didn't like it. So Daddy painted it violet to match her eyes. But the weather turned it purple. Then, when I came home three years ago, he painted it violet again to match my eyes . . . Amy says I have the exact same eyes as Mama."

"Yes, Bessie always said you were the picture of your mother," Pearl agreed.

They were interrupted by a *rat-tat-tat* on the front door. Thinking it might be Esther come back to apologize, Janey dropped the cat on the floor and skipped down the hall. But it was Mr. Potter, the postman. Usually he just slipped the mail through the slot in the door, but this time he held an envelope in his hand. Janey thought it must be another letter from Amy so she reached for it. But Mr. Potter drew it back. "This is special delivery," he said. "I can't release it until it's signed for. Is your uncle home?" Janey shook her head. "Then I guess it's all right if you sign, since I know you're his niece."

Janey signed her name and Mr. Potter gave her the envelope and left without even smiling.

"That's not like Mr. Potter," she thought. "He's usually so friendly." Then she examined the letter in her hand. It was postmarked Toronto, but it wasn't from Amy. And it wasn't for her. It was addressed to her uncle in her father's bold handwriting.

There was a black border around the edge of the envelope that made Janey feel uneasy. And a small voice inside her head told her that this letter was a private family matter. So she slipped it into her pinny pocket and spent the rest of the afternoon helping Pearl Mead make sand cherry tarts and gingersnaps.

Chapter 12

A Letter Edged in Black

*T*he minute her uncle and brother came laughing in the door, and before her uncle even got his hat off, Janey handed him the letter. When he saw the black-edged envelope the smile vanished from his face.

He slit it open with a table knife and withdrew a single sheet of paper. As he read, his forehead creased in a frown.

Janey's stomach knotted and Pearl put a hand on her shoulder. Harry moved a little closer. Then her uncle, with a sad shake of his head, said, "It's a message from your father."

"What does it say?" The knot in Janey's stomach tightened.

"I'm afraid it's bad news, Chicken. Shall I read it to you?"

Janey and Harry both nodded.

Uncle Wallace cleared his throat.

Dear Wallace:

    It is my sad duty to inform you that Gertrude Sarah Davis, my children's maternal grandmother, departed this life Friday last at 3.25 a.m. The old woman succumbed to dropsy. The funeral was held from this house at 2 p.m. the following Monday.

    I would be obliged if you would keep Jane and Harold with you for a while longer until our household is back in order. Patrick and Michael are taking it well, but Amy has been hard hit by the loss of her grandmother.

Regretfully,
John Phair

Wallace Hogan sighed and put the letter on the table.

Harry was first to speak. "What does suckummed mean? And what's dropsy?"

"Dropsy is a bad sickness." Uncle Wallace returned the letter to the envelope. "And succumbed means your gramma died of it."

Sudden tears welled up in Janey's eyes and spilled down her cheeks. Purry-Motor rubbed against her legs in sympathy. She bent down and picked him up. Hiding her face in his fur she mumbled, "I think I'll go to my room now."

"You do that, love." Pearl wiped Janey's cheeks with a corner of her apron. "And I'll stay a while if it's any comfort."

Janey took her father's letter with her and sat on the bed to read it again. Then she curled up on the feather comforter, hugging her cat, and let her tears flow freely. Poor Gramma, she had been ailing ever since Janey could remember. And poor Amy, too. She had had to quit school and take care of Gramma and the whole family just as if she was the mother. Amy had never been able to go out with her friends to parties and picture shows like other seventeen-year-olds.

It was the last words of her father's letter that bothered her the most. "Amy has been hard hit by the loss of her grandmother." What will Amy do now? worried Janey.

Carrying Purry-Motor upside-down, like a furry baby, in her arms, she went back out to the kitchen.

"We have to go home, Harry," she said.

"Why?" Harry scowled at her. "I don't want to go home."

"First you said you didn't want to come to Winnipeg, and now you don't want to go home."

"I didn't say that!"

"You did, too, Harry. You said it on the train. You pouted and whined all the way here."

"Well, I changed my mind. I like it better here now. And our Dad said we could stay as long as Uncle Wallace lets us. Can we stay to the end of summer, Uncle Wallace?"

Wallace Hogan looked into Harry's blue-speckled brown eyes and smiled. "As far as I'm concerned you can stay till the cows come home," he said. Then he turned to Janey. "Why do you feel the need to go home, Chickie? Like Henry says, your father wants you to stay a while. And your gramma's dead and gone now so there's no need to hurry home on her account."

Shifting Purry-Motor to her shoulder, she handed her uncle the letter edged in black. "I'm worried about Amy," she said.

He read it again. Then he scratched his bald spot with his thumbnail. "I see your dilemma," he said. "But maybe I've got the answer."

Janey and Harry looked at him expectantly.

"I could call your father on the blower and ask him how he'd feel about Henry staying on and you making the trip home alone."

"Oh, I don't think he'd mind me travelling alone," Janey's heart thumped in anticipation. "Because I did it once before. But I'm not sure how he'd feel about Harry staying on."

"Huhhh!" Harry huffed. "He won't care. He doesn't even like me."

Uncle Wallace frowned and said, "I'll call him later then."

After supper Papa Wallace glanced at the kitchen clock. "It's six here; that makes it eight in Toronto. Let's see if we can catch your father home."

He picked up the bell-shaped receiver from the hardwood phone-box on the wall and was just about to dial the operator when Janey tugged at his sleeve. Holding the hook down with his finger he gave her a puzzled look. "What is it, Chickie? Are you getting cold feet about travelling alone?"

"No, it's not that."

"What is it then? Spit it out."

"I . . . I . . . I can't bear to leave Purry-Motor." The orange cat was in his favourite place, wrapped around her neck like a fur collar. He bunted his pink nose on her cheek. "If only I could take him with me," she said.

But she didn't think cats were allowed on trains. And Papa Wallace might not want to give him up, and her father would probably say no anyway.

Uncle Wallace pursed his lips and scratched his bald spot again. Then he said, "Well, now, before I call your father, why don't I give the railroad a ring and ask their policy about transporting animals. No use putting the cart before the horse."

"Oh, thank you, Papa. That's such a good idea!" Janey sighed with relief.

The railroad company said that cats and dogs could travel in cages in the baggage car, just so long as their owners looked after them.

"Oh, that wouldn't be a bit of trouble," cried Janey.

"Well, the next go-off is to see what your father says."

Papa Wallace picked up the receiver again and Janey sat on the chair right under the phone-box.

She heard the tinny sound of the operator's voice; then her uncle gave the phone number of the purple house in Toronto. Then he waited. Suddenly his face lit up. "Is that you, Amy-girl?" he shouted over the miles. "This here's your Uncle Wallace. No, no, everything is tip-top here. I'd like a word with your father if you please."

There was a long pause. Janey's heart thumped in her ears and the cat's purring grew louder and louder. "Shhh!" she whispered, cupping her hand over his mouth. Then her uncle began to shout, "Is that you, John Phair? Wallace Hogan here." He stopped to listen. "Oh, we're all fine and dandy,

John. The reason I'm calling is . . . well, your daughter has decided she'd like to come home early and your son, here, would like to stay on a while. How would that sit with you, John?" Uncle Wallace nodded his head and winked down at Janey. "Fine . . . fine . . . now there's just one more thing, John, your daughter would like to bring her cat home with her. No, no, he's always been her cat. Right now he's got a strangle hold around her neck."

Janey could hear the timbre of her father's voice but she couldn't make out what he was saying. "I've already seen to that, John," her uncle explained. "The railroad lets animals travel in the baggage car." He paused again to listen. "Then Jane will leave on the morning train out of Winnipeg, so you can check her arrival at that end. Would you like a word with Henry, John? John? I say, John . . . "

Uncle Wallace frowned at the receiver and hung it up. "I guess we were cut off," he said. "But you've got your wish, Chickie. The cat goes with you. Now let's see about that cage."

❧   ❧   ❧

The minute Harry knew he was staying he flew out the door and up the street to the Pickles' house to tell Eddie the good news. A minute later Essie arrived at the kitchen door.

"I'll miss you, Janey," she said through the screen.

"No, you won't." Janey didn't open the screen door. "You'll still have Irma. Goodbye, Essie. I have to go pack my grip."

Purry-Motor sat on the bed and watched her pack. "I sure hope Norma-Jean hasn't made a new best friend while I've been gone, Purry," Janey said. The cat meowed nervously and jumped into the open grip. "Oh, don't worry, Purry." She lifted him out and kissed him between the ears. "I'm not leaving you this time. You're coming with me."

She felt a little strange about leaving Harry with her Papa Wallace . . . and a little jealous, too, maybe. But she was glad for Harry. He had changed in the few short weeks they'd been here, and she knew the reason why. Harry was right about their father not liking him. She had even heard her father say once, "I could have done without that extra boy." And Harry had heard it, too. She'd never forgotten the hurt look on his face. She knew it was Uncle Wallace's unconditional love that had made the change in Harry.

Chapter 13

Home Again

When they said goodbye at the station, Harry asked Papa Wallace why he didn't wear his Celebration Tie. And Papa replied that saying goodbye to his girl was no cause for celebration. Then Janey cried and Papa cried and even Harry's eyes were misty.

From Union Station, the train headed due north past Provencher Boulevard. Then it turned east and thundered across the Red River Bridge. As Winnipeg receded in the distance, Janey knew, for better or worse, that she was on her way home.

Taking care of her cat in the baggage car kept Janey happy and busy all the long way. The time passed so quickly that she was surprised when the conductor announced: "Next stop Toronto! Toronto's Union Station!"

A trainman helped her off with the cage and her grip and left her standing on the shiny marble floor.

The seething mass of people made both her and the cat jittery. Toronto's Union Station was so much bigger and noisier than Winnipeg's.

She spotted her father easily because he was head and shoulders above the crowd. He was all dressed up in his best suit and necktie and she couldn't help but notice how handsome he was.

"Here I am, Daddy!" she cried.

He strode over and gave her a hug with his big strong arms. "Don't tell me you missed your own flesh-and-blood father," he said, kissing her on the cheek. "I thought you'd have forgot all about me with your 'Papa' Wallace to spoil the lights out of you."

"I missed you a lot, Dad," protested Janey.

"Dad is it?" He looked her up and down with his dark brown eyes. "You've grown up in a hurry."

She laughed and looked around the busy station. "Where's Amy?" She wasn't surprised that her brothers hadn't come to meet her, but she had expected her sister.

Her father frowned. "Amy's been poorly since the old woman pegged out," he said. "But she'll perk up now that you're home, Petty. Come along, then." He picked up her grip and the cage, with the cat cowering on the bottom, and cut a pathway through the crowd. Janey had to run to catch up to him.

On the red wooden streetcar, her father flipped the wicker seatback over and plunked Purry's cage on the seat facing them. All the way home Janey talked a blue streak about Winnipeg. Then she finished up by saying, "Harry says to say hello to you, Dad."

"Oh, he does, does he? But he was in no hurry to come home, was he now?"

"Oh, no, he loves Winnipeg. And he loves Papa Wallace. Papa Wallace says they get along like a house afire."

Her father's black eyebrows bunched together in a frown and suddenly Janey wished she hadn't said that.

"Ah, well, let him be Harry Hogan then, for all I care." He flung his arm around her shoulders and drew her closer to him. "He can stay out there till the moon turns blue, just so long as I've got my Petty back."

The harsh words made Janey cringe. She wished he would miss Harry . . . even a little bit. And she wished he wouldn't call her "Petty" any more.

The minute the purple house came in sight Janey saw that it had a dazzling new coat of paint. It was purpler than ever! Then Amy opened the front door and Janey ran into her arms.

John Phair was in a rare good mood on Janey's first night home. After a special welcome-home supper the family gathered in the parlour. Patrick and Michael sat cross-legged on the floor and Janey sat between her sister and father on the cracked leather davenport. Janey thought how strange it was to be sitting in the very spot where she had last seen her grandmother. The afghan was gone now and the only reminder of her gramma was the cushion she had embroidered with the words "Home Sweet Home."

"Now, Janey, tell us all about Harry." Amy lifted the marmalade cat onto her lap and stroked his thick orange fur. "Are you sure he won't be lonesome all by himself out there?"

"Oh, you don't have to worry about Harry," Janey assured her. "He's the happiest I've ever seen him. Papa Wallace says Henry is the son he never had."

"Henry?" quizzed Amy.

Janey laughed. "That's what Papa always calls him. He can't seem to remember that Harry's real name is Harold."

"Hah!" her father snorted. "What's the matter with the man? Is he so dotty he can't even get his son's name right? And does 'Henry' call Wallace

Hogan 'Papa' same as you do?"

"Sometimes," Janey murmured.

"Ah, well, let Wallace Hogan make a sissy out of him, and the devil take them both."

"Oh, Harry's not a sissy any more, Dad. And Papa Wallace doesn't spoil him. He says he's going to make a man of Harry."

Flinging his arm around Janey's shoulders possessively, he said, "Well, I don't give a fig about 'Henry' just so long as I've got you."

Then he plucked a cigar out of his breast pocket and lit it with a wooden match. "I've been saving this to celebrate your homecoming," he said. Then he dragged three times and sent smoke rings as big as inner tubes floating to the ceiling.

"Do you know what Pearl Mead would say to you, Dad?"

"Who in blazes is Pearl Mead?"

"She's Aunt Bessie's best friend and she always says to Papa — I mean Uncle Wallace — when he lights up his pipe, 'Wallace, if you were meant to smoke the Lord would have put a chimney on your head.'"

Michael and Patrick burst out laughing, but their father didn't think it was funny.

"Well, I say 'Bah!' to Pearl Mead." He stood up, butted out his cigar, put it, still smouldering, into his breast pocket and headed for the front door. Halfway out he called over his shoulder, "I'll be away, then, so don't wait up." And the door shut behind him.

The minute he was gone Mike and Pat leapt up and made a dash towards the kitchen.

"Where do you think you're off to?" called Amy after them.

"Out!" they yelled back. "Bye, Janey, see you tomorrow." And the back door slammed behind them.

Janey felt bewildered. "Where is everybody going, Amy?"

"The boys are probably going to the picture show. They do what they like after he's gone. And I can't blame them. They work hard all week. Mikey delivers for the grocery store and Patty has his paper route. And at the end of the week they give me every penny they earn and I give them back a quarter for spending money."

Then her grey eyes looked darkly at the front door. "But I don't know about *him*."

Him. That's what Gramma used to call their father, but Janey had never heard Amy say it before.

"Is he . . . does he . . . do you think he's gone to the tavern?"

"I don't know. I don't think so. He doesn't smell of beer."

"Well, that's one good thing," Janey sighed. "But I thought they'd all stay home on my first night."

"I thought so, too. That's the least they could do. But never you mind, you've still got me and Purry-Motor." Amy put the slumbering cat in Janey's arms.

Never you mind! Amy sounds more like a mother than a sister, Janey thought, and she's only seventeen.

Chapter 14

Company for Dinner

*N*orma-Jean was thrilled that Janey had come home early. And Janey was thrilled and relieved that Norma hadn't made any new friends since she'd been away.

They were sitting on the back steps of the purple house and Janey let Norma hold Purry-Motor on her lap.

"Oh, Janey, you're so lucky!" Norma buried her freckled face in the cat's orange fur. "I've begged my mother for a kitten but she says we can't have one because their fur makes Lester-de-pester sneeze. But I think he sneezes on purpose, the little brat."

Janey laughed and gazed at Purry like an adoring mother. "But Purry's not a kitten Norma. He's six years old. You're a full-grown marmalade feline, aren't you, Purry?"

Arching his back proudly, he leapt from Norma's lap onto Janey's.

"Let's take him over to Carol Ann's. I want to show him off."

"Oh, haven't you heard? Carol Ann's father lost his job and they had to move to Hamilton to live with her grandmother."

The mention of a grandmother made Janey feel suddenly guilty. She hadn't really missed her gramma yet. In the three years that Janey had lived at home, Amy had always been in charge of Gramma. Janey hadn't had much to do with her. But she decided, out of respect, that she would try to miss her more.

Janey stood up and Purry climbed nimbly to her shoulder and curled around her neck. "C'mon in the house, Norma, and I'll show you postcards of Winnipeg. I bought two of the Golden Boy statue on top of the Legislature Building. One for you and one for Amy."

Just then Amy's pale face appeared at the screen door. "Come in now, Janey," she said in a flat voice.

"Okey-doke. Norma-Jean's coming, too. I want to show her my postcards."

"No. Norma will have to go home now. I need your help."

"Oh, please, Amy! We haven't seen each other for ages and Norma is my best friend."

"I said, no!" snapped Amy. "You come in this minute. And Norma — you go home."

Norma looked as if she had just been slapped.

"Amy didn't mean anything, Norma." Janey explained. "She really likes you."

Norma looked a little happier. "And did you really mean it . . . that I'm your best friend?"

"Yes, I did. Really, really. I'll tell you all about it later. Bye!"

Amy was sitting at the kitchen table poring over Gramma's old cookbook. At her elbow was a big walnut chest. "I want you to polish the silver," she said.

"What silver?" Janey sat down opposite Amy and began kissing the cat's fluffy head.

"Stop slobbering over that creature! It's not sanitary. Put him down this minute. He purrs so loud he gets on my nerves."

Dropping the cat to the floor, Janey stared at Amy in bewilderment. Amy had never been so cross before. And she noticed something else about her sister: she looked messy. Her mousy hair hung in greasy strings around her pale face, and her fingernails were all cracked and dirty. Janey glanced at her own fingernails. They were shaped like pink shells with white half-moons. She smiled, pleased with herself.

"Well!"

"Well, what?"

Amy lifted the lid of the walnut chest. Inside, on red velvet, lay a set of badly tarnished silverware.

"Where did this come from?"

"It was Mama's wedding present from Father."

"Why do I have to clean it? We never use it."

"Well, there's always a first time," snapped Amy.

Janey blinked back the tears. "You could tell me why?" she sniffed.

"Oh, Janey, Janey. I'm sorry!" Amy hugged her sister and stroked her long brown curly hair. "You see, Daddy telephoned to say he was bringing home a lady-friend for supper and we're to set the table in the parlour."

"A lady-friend?" Janey eyebrows flew up like dark wings. "Oh, Amy, it might be fun to have a visitor. Especially a lady."

"Well, if you think it's so much fun, then get busy." Amy shoved a saucer of baking-soda paste and a flannel pad across the table.

By the time she had cleaned several pieces of the silver Janey was dismayed to see that the black tarnish had crept under her fingernails.

Michael and Patrick came in the door together

and Amy ordered them straight upstairs to change their clothes.

"I can't be bothered," said Michael, running his fingers through his sweaty black curls.

"Me neither," agreed Patrick.

All of a sudden Amy whirled around and pitched a potato the size of a baseball. Mike ducked just in time and it bounced off Patty's forehead.

"Oww!" he cried.

"What did you do that for?" demanded Michael.

"Amy . . . what's wrong with you?" cried Janey.

As Amy spun back on her heel, her elbow caught the long handle of a saucepan on the stove. The pot went flying through the air, showering white sauce all over the kitchen, before it crashed to the floor.

The cat howled and streaked under the table; the boys dashed through the parlour and up the stairs. Janey sat stock-still, a half-cleaned knife in her hand. Amy sank, with a moan, into a chair and buried her face in her arms.

Janey's heart swelled with concern for her sister. Throwing her arms around her she whispered, "Don't worry, Amy. Pearl Mead always says 'things are never so bad they couldn't be worse.' At least the sauce wasn't hot. I'll help you clean up and make another supper."

Amy raised a tragic face. "Thank you, Janey. But it's too late to make another supper."

"No, it's not. First we'll clean up, then you can make Gramma's Scotch hash. And we'll eat right here in the kitchen."

"He said the parlour."

"Well, if the lady's nice she won't mind the kitchen. And if she's not nice, then who cares?"

Together they cleaned up the mess. Then Janey happily put the half-polished silver away and set the kitchen table with the everyday dishes and cutlery. Next she ran outside and picked a nosegay of buttercups and daisies and put them in a pint milk bottle and sat it in the middle of the green-checkered oilcloth.

The Scotch hash was simmering in the covered saucepan when they heard the front door open. "Hello, the house!" called out their father.

Janey saw Amy's back stiffen. "We're in the kitchen, Daddy!" she called back.

He came striding through the parlour into the kitchen, followed by a tall, pretty woman. His black eyebrows bunched in a frown when he saw the kitchen table set. Marching over to the stove he lifted the lid off the saucepan and demanded, "Is this what we're having?"

Janey was just about to open her mouth when

the lady standing in the doorway sniffed the air and said, "Mmm, something smells delicious."

Amy turned her head slightly and glanced at the visitor out of the corner of her eye. Janey heard her give a little gasp, and she knew exactly why. The lady had chestnut brown hair and violet-blue eyes and she was wearing a pink flowered dress. She looked just like the portrait of their mother in the oval frame on the wall of their father's den!

Just then Michael and Patrick came downstairs.

"Children!" John Phair clapped his big hands together. "May I present my good friend, Mrs. Elinor Flowers."

Mrs.! Janey saw a relieved look cross Amy's face.

"Elinor. I'd like you to meet my family: this is Amy, my right-hand man, and this here is Michael, my number one son, and Patrick, number two son, and last but not least, my pretty little Petty."

"Oh, please, Daddy, don't call me that." Janey held out her hand to the lady. "My name is Jane Elizabeth Phair," she said.

"I stand corrected," grinned her father. Mrs. Flowers smiled and shook hands with each of them. Except Amy, who had turned back to the stove.

"Well, that's the lot," their father said.

"Oh, no, Daddy!" Janey contradicted. "That's not the lot. You forgot our Harry."

"Ah, yes. 'Henry.' Well, since he's chosen to live a thousand miles away with his uncle by marriage . . . then so much for Henry."

"Would everyone please sit down," said Amy. "I'm about to serve the supper."

"Oh, do let me help you, dear," offered Elinor Flowers.

"No, thank you, *Mrs*. Flowers. Janey will help me. And Michael . . . Patrick . . . you can tuck the chairs up to the table."

"And what would you have me do, Vinny?" John Phair asked in a wheedling tone, using the pet name he knew she loved because it was her mother's.

"Do as you always do, Father." The chill in Amy's voice made Janey's skin crawl. "Sit down and wait to be served."

Shaking his head with a puzzled frown, he pulled out the chair on his right-hand side. "You sit here beside me, Elinor," he said.

Hmmm, Janey thought. He calls her by her first name.

"The table looks lovely," Mrs. Flowers commented.

"That's nice you thought of a nosegay, Vinny," remarked their father.

"It was Janey's idea. Not mine," answered Amy coldly. Then she set the steaming bowl in front of him and took her place at the opposite end of the table.

Instead of serving only himself, as he usually did, he served their guest first, then the children, and himself last.

"Mmmm." Savouring the first mouthful, Mrs. Flowers said, "It's the best stew I've ever tasted. You'll have to give me your recipe, Amy."

Amy didn't answer so Janey piped up, "Oh, it's not stew, Mrs. Flowers. It's Gramma's Scotch hash. Our Amy is the best cook in the world. She's even better than Aunt Bessie was."

"And who is Aunt Bessie?" asked Mrs. Flowers brightly.

"Bessie was sister to my late wife," John Phair explained. "She took our Janey to Winnipeg and raised her from babyhood. Then, when Bessie passed over, three years ago, our Janey came home to live with her rightful family."

Janey had heard this explanation before. But this time the words "late wife" stuck in her mind like a needle in a pincushion. She glanced at Amy and saw that her sister's face had gone the colour of putty.

Mrs. Flowers discreetly changed the subject. "Tell me all about your holiday out west, Jane," she said.

Janey started talking a mile a minute about everything and everybody in Winnipeg.

"Janey!" Amy snapped. "Hush up and eat your supper."

"But . . . Elinor asked . . . "

"Don't you mean *Mrs. Flowers?*"

"Oh, I'm sorry, Mrs. Flowers," Janey apologized. "I forgot you're a married lady."

Elinor Flowers patted her mouth with her napkin. "There's no need to apologize, my dear," she said quietly. "And actually I'm a widow. My husband, Roger, was killed at Vimy Ridge."

Her voice was so sad that Janey quickly asked another question. "Have you got any children?"

"No." Mrs. Flowers looked at John Phair. "Your father is luckier than I in that respect. But perhaps he'll be willing to share."

In the silence that followed her remark you could have heard a pin drop. Then, as if on cue, a big ball of orange fluff came sailing from the top of the cabinet and landed on Janey's shoulder.

"Ohhh!" cried Mrs. Flowers. "What a gorgeous creature."

"Janey!" scolded Amy. "You know that cat is not allowed near the table."

"Shoo!" John Phair smacked his hands together like a thunderclap, scaring the wits out of Purry-

Motor. Leaping from Janey's shoulder he landed in the middle of the table, knocking over the pint bottle. Water and flowers spewed across the oilcloth.

"I'm sorry! I'm sorry!" cried Janey, mopping frantically with her napkin.

"Here, let me help you." Mrs. Flowers started mopping, too. "Water won't hurt oilcloth, so there's no harm done."

Suddenly John Phair burst out laughing. His laughter was such a relief that they all joined in. All except Amy. But even Amy's sour face couldn't dampen Janey's spirits. And she couldn't take her eyes off Elinor Flowers.

Chapter 15

Getting to Know Her

"*I* wonder how long Daddy has been keeping company with Elinor." Janey clasped her hands behind her head on the pillow.

Amy hadn't played the piano that night. Instead she had come to bed early. Opening the bedroom window, she propped it up with a stick and slipped into bed beside her sister.

"*Mrs. Flowers*," she corrected. "And how should I know."

"Well, did he ever mention her before?"

"No. But I've certainly noticed him getting all gussied up on Saturday nights. And weeknights, too. And he bought himself two new neckties and a pinstriped shirt when both boys need new shoes. And he's been working days at the shop lately when he used to prefer the night shift."

Amy flicked off the lamp and flopped over on

her side. "Goodnight, Janey," she said.

"Goodnight, Amy." Janey laced her fingers across her stomach and thought about the whole evening. Picturing Elinor's face made her smile.

"Daddy was in a really good mood tonight, so maybe it's nice he's got a girlfriend," she said.

Amy flounced over so hard the bedsprings squawked. "Don't you *dare* call that woman his girlfriend. How could our father even look at another woman after our mother?"

"But . . . but . . . Mama's been dead for a long time now, Amy."

"Shut . . . up . . . Jane! Shut up and go to sleep this instant."

Cringing at the harsh words, Janey pulled herself over to the far edge of the mattress and lay as still as she could.

Suddenly, she flung back the cover, crawled down the length of the bed and climbed off, scraping her leg on the bottom rail. "Ouch!" she cried, rubbing her shin and stamping her foot on the floor.

Amy bounced up and switched on the lamp. "What on earth are you doing?" she asked crossly.

"I scratched my leg and I've got a cramp in my little toe and I have to go to the bathroom." Janey was half crying as she stomped out of the room.

When she came back Amy was sitting up in bed

with their mother's picture in her hands. Janey crawled back in and leaned her cheek on Amy's arm. "She looks a lot like her, doesn't she?" she whispered.

"Like who?"

"Oh, Amy, you know who. Mrs. Flowers. They've got the same brown wavy hair and violet-coloured eyes. Probably that's why Daddy likes her."

"He hasn't known her long enough to like her," Amy snapped. "And Mrs. Flowers' hair is bobbed too short to resemble Mama's. And why are you whispering? Gramma's not across the hall any more, you know."

"I know. I guess I can't believe she's really gone because I wasn't here to say goodbye."

Amy set the picture back on the washstand and pulled the chain of the Tiffany lamp. "I'm sorry, Janey," she said. "Now go to sleep like a good girl."

They turned back to back and lay quietly for a while. But Janey couldn't stop thinking. "I wonder why she hasn't got any children?" she said.

Amy didn't answer.

Janey turned over on her back and cupped her hands behind her head again. "I wish Purry-Motor could sleep with me," she said. "Aunt Bessie let him sleep with me. Ever since the time he saved my life."

Amy shot bolt upright, switched on the lamp and

punched her pillow. "All right, tell me about it. And it better be good."

Janey hoisted up on her elbows. "Well, it was the time Essie Pickles and me got lost in the woods."

"Essie Pickles and I . . . and this better be a true story."

"Oh, it is, I promise. We were playing house in Essie's backyard when we decided to go for a walk in the forest to pick a nosegay of wildflowers for our table."

"A forest? In Winnipeg?"

"Well, it was really a park but we thought it was a forest because it was full of trees. Well, there's a gate in the middle of their back fence but the latch was too high for us to reach. We were only little — we didn't go to school yet. So we dragged over the garbage pail and I climbed up on it and undid the latch."

"Janey. I've got a big wash to do tomorrow and I need my sleep. So tell me, what has picking flowers got to do with the cat saving your life?"

"I'm coming to that. Well . . . "

"Stop saying well, well, well, and get to the point, or this story is finished."

"Well . . . sorry . . . Purry-Motor had come with us and he was having lots of fun climbing up trees and chasing butterflies, while we were picking ladybells and jack-in-the-pulpits. Then all of a sudden Essie looked scared and said, 'I want to go home' and I said 'me too.' But the trouble was I didn't know which way was home. Well, we wandered up and down pathways for ages and Essie started to cry and yell, 'We're lost! We're lost! We're lost!' And I was getting scared, too, because I knew we were in a terrible dilemma . . . but I didn't know that word way back then."

Amy's lips twitched and she said, "Go on."

"Well . . . we wandered round and round for hours and I was just about to burst out crying myself when Purry-Motor jumped out of a tree and landed right at my feet. Well . . . sorry . . . he looked up at me with his big gold eyes . . . did you ever notice that Purry's eyes are gold, not green like ordinary cats?"

Amy frowned and Janey hurried on. "He me-owed really loud and started walking away waving his tail like a flag. So I said to Essie, 'I think he wants us to follow him,' so we did. He kept glancing back over his shoulder to make sure we were there. Well, by the time we came in sight of Essie's back fence we heard Mrs. Pickles and Aunt Bessie calling our names hysterically. So we ran to tell them that Purry-Motor had saved our lives. But before we could say one word Essie's mother grabbed her and spanked her bottom all the way into their house and Aunt Bessie grabbed me by the pigtail and she marched me home."

By this time Amy was smiling in spite of herself. "Did Aunt Bessie spank you, too? You certainly deserved it."

"Oh, no. Aunt Bessie didn't believe in spanking. And when I told her how Purry-Motor had saved our lives she gave him an extra saucer of milk for his supper. And for punishment she sent me to bed early. But before I went to sleep I heard her telling Papa Wallace what Purry had done. And he said, 'And folks say dogs are smarter than cats!' And ever after that Purry was allowed to sleep in my bed."

"Is that the end?"

"Yes. But if you want another cat story I've got lots more."

"No, thanks. I've heard enough for one night. But I hope you wrote it down in your copybook, Janey. It's a really good story."

Amy got up, then, and padded barefoot down the stairs. She came back carrying the big fat marmalade cat. Plunking him down on the bed, she clicked off the light.

Purry turned round and round in circles and finally settled into a ball between them. In seconds he started to purr. The purring grew louder and louder until he sounded like Papa Wallace's tin lizzie the time the muffler fell off.

"Shhh!" Janey whispered in his ear. She was afraid Amy would change her mind. Then she heard a muffled giggle.

"Goodnight, Amy," she ventured.

"Goodnight, Janey. And goodnight to you, too, Noisy-Motor."

At last Janey fell asleep and she began to dream. She dreamt she was a little girl again playing in Essie's backyard. But Essie wasn't Essie . . . she was Norma-Jean. And Aunt Bessie, who was talking over the fence to Mrs. Pickles, wasn't Aunt Bessie any more, she was Elinor Flowers.

Chapter 16

Harry's Question

*A*ll the leaves on the maple tree in front of the purple house had changed from green to red before a letter finally arrived from Harry.

"I left it for you to open, Janey." Amy was washing woolens with Lux soap flakes in a basin in the sink. "Why don't you read it to me."

"Okey-doke!"

"What does okey-doke mean?"

"It means yes."

"If it means yes, then say yes."

"Okey-doke." Janey tore open the envelope.

> *Winnipeg, Manitoba,*
> *September 30, 1931.*

Dear Everybody:

Papa Wallace says I should write you a letter. So here it is. I am in the same class as

Eddie Pickles at Elmer Street School. I like it fine.

On Saturdays Papa lets me help in his furniture shop. He pays me fifteen cents. He says I have a knack for woodwork. Manual Training is my favourite subject in school.

Excuse my wiggly writing but Pearl Mead is jiggling the table. She is rolling dough for gooseberry pies. Pearl says she misses you, Janey. Papa Wallace wants to know how Purry-Motor is doing. He also gave me your room, Janey. I hope you don't mind.

Why I am really writing this letter is to ask our dad an important question: can I stay out here with Papa Wallace forever? Uncle Wallace says he will give Dad a call on the blower.

I have one more thing to tell you, then I will go because Eddie Pickles and Shorty Miller and Percy Pinch are waiting for me to play stick hockey while it's still light out.

I think this will make you laugh, Janey, and you can write it into a story if you like. Last Tuesday me and the gang were walking along Main Street and we came to Papa's shop. On the door was a note which said, "Be back later." I tried the door but it was locked.

*Well, Percy Pinch asked me how come
there were no coffins in the window if it was
a coffin shop. I had already asked Pearl
Mead that and she said it would not be in
good taste to have them on show, so that's
what I told Percy. Then he said he bet my
uncle didn't even make coffins so I took them
around the back to look in the cellar window.
Well, the window wasn't locked so I pushed it
open and we all jumped in. There were two
coffins on the worktables. One was finished
and the other one wasn't even shellacked yet.
Then Shorty dared me to get in the finished
one and try it on for size. So I did.*

"I can't believe our timid little Harry would do
such a thing," marvelled Amy.

"I told you he's changed," said Janey. Then she
read on:

*I laid my head on the pillow and closed
my eyes and held my breath so I would look
dead. Well, I must have done a good job
because Percy Pinch let out a scream and
slammed down the lid. And I heard the latch
go click! It was black as coal in there so I
started pushing on the lid. But guess what?
It wouldn't budge. I was locked in. So I
started hollering my head off. The guys tried*

to pry the lid open but they couldn't so they yelled through the lid that they'd go and get help and they left me to smother in there. Well, lucky for me Papa Wallace had just drove up and they told him where I was and the next thing I knew the lid flew open and Papa grabbed a handful of my shirt and hauled me out. I never saw him so mad and I was sure he was going to send me home on the next train. That's when I knew how bad I wanted to stay.

I said I was sorry but he wouldn't speak to me for hours. Then all of a sudden he slapped his knee and let out a big snort. You know how Papa snorts when he laughs, Janey. Then he told me he played the same trick when he was a boy (his uncle was the coffin-maker back then) but he didn't get caught. Then he asked me did I find the coffin comfy. And I said, heck no, it was hard as a brick. And he said, that's because he hadn't put the mattress in yet. And I said, why would a dead person need a mattress? And he said they don't, but it's a comfort to their folks, and he only charges two dollars extra. I said that sounded like a good deal and he slapped his knee and snorted again and said

I was a chip off the old block. Then he made
me promise never to do that again and I never
will. You can bet your shirt on that!

Your son and brother,
~~Henry~~*Harold Phair.*

Amy laughed as she squeezed the rinse water
out of Janey's blue woolen tam and stretched it over
a dinner plate. "I'm not too sure Father will think
Harry's shenanigans are as funny as Uncle Wallace
did," she said as she balanced the plate on two glass
jars on the sink-board.

"I hate that tam," Janey said, screwing up her
nose.

"Why? It's a nice blue tam, and your gramma
knit it for you."

"It's not blue, it's purple, and when I wear it the
boys call me Blueberry Pie."

"Oh, don't pay any attention to them. They're
silly. But about Harry's letter . . . I'm concerned
what Father will say."

"Well, let's not show it to him, then. Harry said
that Uncle Wallace is going to call him on the
blower, anyway."

"We can't do that. He asked me just yesterday if
we had any word from Harry."

Wiping her water-wrinkled hands on her apron,

Amy set up the ironing board between two chairs. When the iron was hot she started ironing her father's pinstriped shirt.

Janey knew her father expected his shirt to be ready at a moment's notice. And she could tell by the way Amy thumped the iron down on the metal stand that she resented the job.

≥ ≥ ≥

The minute her father came in the door Janey ran to meet him. "Guess what, Daddy! There's a letter from Harry."

"It's high time," he said, coming into the kitchen. "I begun to think Wallace Hogan had kidnapped the boy. What's he got to say for himself?"

"Do you want me to read it to you?" If he said yes, she could skip the part about the coffin.

"No. I got twenty-twenty eyesight. I'm not an old codger that needs to be read to. Give it here."

Janey handed him the letter with a quick glance at Amy. "Set the table," Amy said. "Michael and Patrick will be home any minute."

Sliding the plates around the oilcloth like playing cards, Janey kept glancing at her father trying to read his mind.

When he had finished the letter she was surprised to see that his eyes were twinkling. "Why, that young whippersnapper," he chortled. "I didn't think he had it in him. He's a chip off the old block all right, but if Wallace Hogan thinks it's off *his* block he's got another think coming. Harry's no flesh and blood of his."

*a. *a. *a.

After supper, when Janey was studying at one end of the table and Amy was folding clothes at the other, their father looked up from his newspaper and said, "What do you think, Vinny?"

"About what, Father?"

"About young 'Henry' staying out there 'forever' with Wallace Hogan."

"I think it would be good for Harry," Amy said.

John Phair frowned and scanned the letter again. Then he looked at Janey. "What about you, Petty, what do you think?"

"I think the same as Amy, Daddy. Just so long as . . ."

"Just so long as what?"

"Just so long as Harry knows he can come home whenever he wants to."

Folding the letter he stuffed it back into its envelope. "He should know that already," he muttered.

"Well, he'll know even better if you tell him."

The words were hardly out of her mouth when the phone rang.

Her father picked up the receiver and bellowed, "John Phair, here!" Janey heard the operator talking then, after a short pause, she recognized her uncle's voice speaking extra loud to cover the distance. "There's no need to shout, Wallace," her father snapped. "I can hear you plain as if you were next door." He changed the earpiece from one side to the other and listened intently. Then he asked to speak to Harry.

"Is that you, Harold? So you've decided to stay out there in no-man's land have you?" Harry must have said yes, because his father continued, "Well, just so you know that if you ever get fed up with living amongst coffins and caskets you've always got a proper home to come back to." He listened, then said, "You're welcome. Goodbye," and hung up.

"There." He looked Janey straight in the eye. "Are you satisfied?" But instead of waiting for an answer he took his shirt from the neat pile of ironing, went into his den, changed his clothes and left without another word.

Janey had hoped to say hello to Harry and her uncle. With a big sigh, she closed her history book.

"What's the sigh for?" Amy asked.

"I'm missing Harry and Papa and Pearl."

"Well, Father told Harry exactly what you asked him to. What more do you want?"

"I don't know. I just feel as if I should be there, too."

"But . . . you belong here with us."

"I don't know *where* I belong."

"Well, it was your own choice to come home." Amy gathered up the clothes and left the room in a huff.

Chapter 17

Fall Cleaning

"Saturday, October 30, 1931," Janey wrote in her workbook. She had been studying at the parlour table since early morning.

Amy had just finished damp-mopping the linoleum runner that ran straight through the parlour from the front door to the kitchen. She stopped and leaned her chin on the mop handle. "I've a good mind to tackle that room," she said.

Janey looked to see what room she was talking about. Amy's eyes were fixed on the den door.

"Daddy's den?"

"Yes, Daddy's den."

Janey shook her head. "He'll be mad," she said.

"Well, what's the use of fall house-cleaning if one room never gets done?" Poking a loose strand of hair under her dustcap, Amy eased the den door open. She wrinkled her nose at the smell that seeped out. "It's a pigsty in there," she said.

Janey wiped her pen-nib on a pink blotter, screwed the lid back on the ink bottle, and put the blotter in her arithmetic book so she wouldn't lose her place. "I'll help you," she said.

"No, Janey, keep at your studies. I don't want you to be a charwoman like me when you're seventeen. I expect you to be in Normal School by then."

"Isn't Normal School for teachers? I don't want to be a teacher, I want to be a writer."

"Well, you can be both if you set your mind to it."

"But I'm tired of studying." She rubbed her eyes with her fists.

"Oh, all right. You can help for a little while, to give your eyes a rest. Go get the lemon oil from the kitchen."

Janey was bent over double searching for the lemon oil under the sink when a piercing cry from the den made her jump and crack her skull on the edge of the porcelain sink. Grabbing her head, her heart pounding, she ran to see what was the matter.

Amy was standing as still as a statue pointing to a clean oval space on the wall. "Our mother's picture." She choked on the words. "Where is our mother's picture?"

Janey stared at the space on the wall. "Maybe it

fell down and Daddy hasn't had time to put it back up," she said. "Let's look for it."

Dropping to her hands and knees, she looked under the bed. Strewn under there were bottles and newspapers and dirty socks and dust-balls the size of her fist. But no picture.

Just then she heard her father pounding up the veranda steps. He was singing in his loud baritone: "Potatoes are cheaper, tomatoes are cheaper, now's the time to fall in love!" Jumping to her feet, she stood beside Amy at the den door.

She expected him to be mad because they were in his room, but to her surprise he gave them a great big smile. "Well, now, it must be true that great minds think alike," he declared. "I was just about to ask for some help with my cleanup."

Janey darted a sidelong glance at her sister. Amy's eyes were as cold and grey as the lake in winter. Raising her hand slowly, she pointed to the space on the wall. "Does your cleanup include throwing away my mother's picture?" she dared to ask.

Anger fell like a mask over their father's face. "Get away from me, the both of you," he snarled. He pushed them roughly out the door and slammed it behind them.

Janey gathered her books off the parlour table

and tiptoed after Amy into the kitchen. She tried to finish her arithmetic assignment but she couldn't keep her mind on fractions.

Suddenly the den door flew open again and out stomped their father. Pointedly ignoring them, he tramped through the kitchen and down the cellar stairs. Back he came with an armload of corrugated boxes.

For several hours they heard him in the den, banging and thumping and swearing. Then there was a long silence.

Suddenly the phone rang and the girls nearly jumped out of their skins.

"I'll get it!" cried Janey. Glad for the interruption, she grabbed the receiver off the hook before it could ring again. A strange man's voice said, "Is Mr. John Phair there?"

"Yes, my dad's here. Who wants to know? Oh . . . just a minute please." She let the receiver dangle down the wall and looked at Amy. Amy inclined her head toward the parlour.

Janey had her fist up, ready to knock on the den door, when she changed her mind. Leaning down, she cupped her hands around the keyhole. "Daddy, you're wanted on the phone."

No answer.

"Daddy!"

"Who the blazes is it?"

"It's me, Janey."

"I know who you are. Who wants me on the phone?"

"A man. He says his name is Mr. Gower."

Bolting out the door, her father brushed past her and snatched up the receiver. "John Phair here!" he shouted. As he listened, the scowl on his face turned into an excited grin. "Hold the fort, I'll be right there!" Then he slammed up the phone, grabbed his coat from the rack and rushed out the front door.

Michael nearly collided with him on the purple steps. Jumping aside, he watched his father go galloping up the street.

"Where's he going?" he asked.

"We don't know," Janey said. "A man named Mr. Gower phoned him and Daddy said 'Hold the fort' and he left."

"Why is the door to his den open? It stinks in there."

"Then close it," snapped Amy.

His hand on the knob, Michael peered inside. "Hey, there's boxes filled with junk all over the place. It looks like he's moving."

"No, he's not moving. He's just cleaning up," Janey explained.

"Too bad," said Michael.

Chapter 18

Black Beauty

*T*he family was sitting around the kitchen table glumly eating their soup when the silence was shattered by an ear-splitting Ahhh-ooo-gaaa! from the street.

"What the heck is that?" cried Michael. Leaping up, he bolted through the parlour and out the front door with Patrick and Janey right at his heels.

There at the curb was a shiny black motor-car and, sitting proud as punch behind the wheel, was their beaming father.

"Get out here, the lot of you!" he hollered.

Janey squealed and clapped her hands as she ran down the steps. "It's a Model T just like Uncle Wallace's," she cried.

"This here is no tin lizzie, girl!" her father snorted. "This here is a Durante see-dan. Isn't she a beauty?"

"Yes, a Black Beauty!" Janey cried. And so the car was christened.

Janey ran around the car and bounced from the running board onto the leather seat beside her father. The two boys hopped in the back.

Sliding her hand along the shiny wood dashboard, Janey asked, "Whose car is it, Daddy?"

"It's my car, Petty. It's our car. No more streetcars for John Phair's family." Then he looked up to the veranda where Amy was standing with her hands on the railing.

Her father blasted the horn again. "It's calling you, Vinny!" he teased.

Still she didn't budge so he released the brake and shifted the gear-stick. The car began to roll.

Suddenly Amy cried, "Wait for me!" and she leapt down the purple steps, leaving the door wide open. Squeezing in beside Janey, she touched the smooth leather seat between them. "Is it a brand-new car, Father?"

"Well, now." His forehead furrowed. "Its a 1929 Durante. Best car on the market."

Then he tramped on the gas and careered around the neighborhood, the tires squealing. People poured out of their houses to see who was lucky enough to have a brand new car in these hard times.

"I didn't know you had a driving license, Dad,"

shouted Mikey over the roar of the engine.

"License be hanged. Why would a man need a license to operate his own vehicle?"

That makes sense, Janey thought. Then she waved proudly at the gawping kids along the curb.

"If it's not brand new, Dad, who owned it before?" shouted Patrick from the back seat.

"Well . . . Dan Gower, the man who sold it to me, assured me that it belonged to a little old lady who only drove it on Sundays," his father shouted back. "So it's good as new at half the price!"

That makes sense, too, Janey thought. Daddy sure is smart.

After a breathtaking ride they came to a jolting stop back in front of the purple house.

Their dad ate his supper in a big hurry that night and scraped back his chair. "Is my pinstripe ready, Amy?" he asked, his voice still kindled with excitement.

"I put it away in your top drawer, Daddy," Janey said.

"Thank you, Petty." He pinched her cheek and disappeared into his den. A few minutes later he reappeared, looking as if he had just stepped out of a band-box. Donning his coat and hat, he called over his shoulder, "I'll be away, now. Don't wait up!" and the door clapped shut behind him.

Janey dashed to the parlour window and peeked through the curtains just in time to see the practically new Durante darting up the street.

"I knew it." Amy had come up behind her.

"Knew what?" asked Janey.

"It's not for us. It's for *her*."

Janey knew exactly who Amy meant by *her*. "But it's for us, too," she insisted as they walked back to the kitchen. If only Amy wasn't so dead-set against Elinor Flowers. "And Daddy works hard, so why shouldn't he have a car?" she said. She wanted to add, "And why shouldn't he have a lady-friend, too," but she didn't dare.

"Humph!" grumbled Amy, sounding just like Gramma Davis. "It would be more to his credit if he bought something useful. Like an electric washing-machine, for instance. Mrs. Plum has a Thor electric and she says her clothes come out spotless."

Janey glanced over to the corner at the old wooden washer. The name Acme painted on the side was almost worn right off. She pictured, first Gramma, then Amy, working the hand-powered lever back and forth for endless hours every wash-day. Amy was right, of course. An electric washing machine would be more to her father's credit, but not nearly so much fun, she thought, as a practically new motor-car.

Chapter 19

Mrs. Flowers

*F*or two whole weeks Mrs. Flowers' name wasn't even mentioned in the purple house, and Janey began to worry that her dad and Mrs. Flowers weren't friends any more.

By the second Saturday Janey was determined to find out what was going on. She was standing on the front porch shaking the cedar mop over the railing when her father came striding up the sidewalk with a long Tip Top Tailors box under his arm. He only worked half-days on Saturdays and he didn't take his car to work. Most people who owned a car didn't drive it in wintertime. As soon as November came they took the wheels off and set the car up on wooden blocks and covered it with a tarpaulin to wait for spring. But her dad hadn't done that yet. Black Beauty was still parked beside the curb in front of the house.

"Hello, Daddy." She held the mop still so he wouldn't get dust in his face. "How's Mrs. Flowers?"

He paused on the top step. "Who wants to know?" he asked suspiciously.

"I do. I miss her."

"Ahh." He smiled at her approvingly. "She's fine. She's very fine. She misses you, too, Petty."

"Does that mean you've seen her lately?"

He turned with his hand on the door latch. "Yes. As a matter of fact I had lunch with her this week."

"You had lunch! At her house?"

"No. She's not got a house. She lives in a flat over top the Red Rose Cafe on Gerrard Street. It's not far from Lever Brothers, so I eat there sometimes. That's where we met."

"Ohhh!" They met at the Red Rose Cafe. It sounds romantic, Janey thought as she followed him into the house.

Hanging up his coat he glanced around the parlour. "Where's your sister? Why are you doing the cedar mopping today?"

"Oh, I'm just doing it for a change from homework. Usually Amy won't allow me to do housework. 'Schoolwork comes first,' she says. I have to get the education she never got. Right now she's lying down with a sick headache."

Her father frowned at the mention of Amy's schooling, or lack of it. "She needs to see a doctor," he said. Then he went into his den and closed the door.

At five o'clock, when the house was tidy, Janey was back at her books and Amy was in the kitchen making supper, her father came out of his den all spruced up again. But this time he was sporting, not only his pinstriped shirt and necktie, but a brand new overcoat and green felt fedora.

"Daddy!" Janey's big blue eyes stretched with admiration. "You look handsomer than Buck Jones." Buck Jones was her and Norma's favourite cowboy star. They had seen him in *Silver Spurs* at the Beaches show down on Queen Street.

"Well, thank you, Petty," he said, pulling on black gloves that smelled of new leather. "And how are you feeling today, Vinny?"

Amy turned from the sink and wiped her hands on her apron. "Aren't you going to be home for supper again, Father?"

Snapping the brim of his new fedora down over his right eye, he said, "I asked for your health, Vinny."

"I'm fine, thank you."

"Then I'll be away, so don't wait up."

Janey ran to the front window to watch him

through the curtains. She could hear the *Rrrrum,*
rrrum, rrrum, as her father tried to start the car.
But the cold engine refused to turn over.

Just then Patty came along with his newspaper bag slung over his shoulder. Dropping his bag
on the sidewalk, he said, "Gimme the crank, Dad,
and I'll start it for you!" It took three mighty
swings of the crank before the engine roared into
life and Black Beauty went lurching down the
street.

Patty came in looking proud as punch of himself.
"Good for you, Patty!" Janey said. Then she added,
"Didn't Daddy look handsome today?"

Patty shrugged and Michael, who was stroking
his chin looking for whiskers at the kitchen mirror,
said, "Who's better looking, him or me?"

Janey laughed and said, "You are, Michael.
Norma-Jean thinks you're handsome as a movie
star. But don't tell Daddy I said so."

Then Amy muttered, "He bought *himself* new
clothes!"

"Well, he needs new clothes sometimes," Janey
protested.

"We all need new clothes," Amy said darkly.

"Oh, but Amy, Daddy looks so handsome in that
green fedora."

"Handsome is as handsome does," grumbled

Amy. Then she turned on Michael. "Get yourself away from that looking glass and go down cellar to check the furnace. I don't think he even looked at it before he went out gallivanting."

Chapter 20

A Chance Meeting

"What does she look like — your dad's lady-friend, Janey?" Janey had confided in her best friend for the first time about Mrs. Flowers, and Norma-Jean was all agog.

"Don't you dare forget, Norma, that it's a secret. If you tell anybody else I'll never speak to you again."

"Oh, I won't tell, cross my heart." Norma shifted her schoolbag from her right hand to her left so she could cross her heart properly.

They were on their way to White's Drug Store on Queen Street. They had saved their milk money that day so they could treat themselves.

Hopping up on the wobbly bar stools they watched in fascination as Mr. White huffed his steamy breath on the tall soda glasses and polished them to a sparkling shine on his spotty apron.

"What'll it be, boys?" He greeted them with the same old worn-out joke he'd used for years. Janey laughed in spite of herself. When she was a little girl she really believed that Mr. White didn't know the difference.

"I'll have a chocolate soda, please," she said.

"Me, too," agreed Norma.

Their mouths watered as he plopped two scoops of ice-cream and two squirts of chocolate sauce into the jar of soda-water. Then he screwed on the lid and shook it for all he was worth. Next he poured the thick chocolate foam into the glasses he had just polished on his apron and stood two straws upright in the middle of each.

"That'll be five dollars," he said with a straight face. They snickered and put their nickels on the marble counter.

Between sucks on the paper straws Norma-Jean whispered, "Tell me more about Mrs. Flowers."

"Well . . . " Janey took a long delicious suck that collapsed her straw. She wished she could break herself of the habit of saying "well" all the time because it got on Amy's nerves. But then, everything seemed to get on Amy's nerves lately. "Well, I think my sister is afraid that Mrs. Flowers might become my father's girlfriend."

"Really!" Norma's mouth dropped open so far

that Janey could see her chocolaty tonsils. "But . . . didn't you just call her *Mrs.*?"

"Yes, but she's not married any more. Her husband got killed at Vimy Ridge. She's a war widow."

"Ohhh!" Norma's green eyes grew as big and round as Little Orphan Annie's. "Do you think your dad might marry her?"

Janey nearly choked on her soda. "Oh, Norma, don't even think that! Amy would just die if that happened."

Just then Janey noticed Mr. White cocking his head in their direction, so she leaned her brown curly head closer to Norma's red mop and lowered her voice to a breathy whisper.

The bell over the door jangled, and another customer came in. Janey was facing the door and when she saw who it was she bit her tongue by mistake. "Don't look now," she whispered, pinching her stinging tongue, "but if Pearl Mead was here she'd say, 'speak of the devil.'"

Norma swivelled her head around like an owl and stared straight into the violet eyes of Mrs. Elinor Flowers.

"Well, fancy meeting you here!" Mrs. Flowers came straight to Janey's side.

"Hello, Mrs. Flowers." Janey coughed to clear her throat.

"Not Mrs., dear. Call me Elinor. Unless, of course, you want me to call you Miss Phair."

Janey giggled and Elinor hopped up on the empty stool beside her. Placing her briefcase on the counter beside her, she stripped off her grey kid gloves and laid them on top. Then she undid her fur collar. It was a little red fox, and when she snapped open his mouth he let go of his tail. "Aren't you going to introduce me to your friend?"

"Oh, sure. This is my best friend, Norma-Jean Cox. Norma, this is Mrs. Flowers . . . I mean Elinor."

Mrs. Flowers reached across Janey to shake hands with Norma-Jean. Then she said, "Do you girls mind if I join you, or would I be interrupting secrets?"

"We had composition but I'm not very good at it," admitted Norma. "Janey is the best story writer in our class."

"What did you write about, Jane?"

"Oh, just another cat story. I write lots of cat stories because of Purry-Motor, but I'm starting to run out of ideas."

Mr. White brought the sodas and Mrs. Flowers gave him three nickels and he gave her a wink.

"Well, I've got a cat story for you." Mrs. Flowers smiled dreamily as she dunked her straw up and down in the thick soda. "It happened in 1916, while my Roger was on embarkation leave."

Janey noticed her bottom lip quivering. She asked quickly, "What's embarkation leave?"

Shaking off her sudden melancholy, Mrs. Flowers continued. "It's a soldier's last leave before being sent overseas," she explained. "We were newlyweds and we had just moved into our first home, a cold-water flat on Russett Avenue here in Toronto. Our landlady, Mrs. Brigham, who lived downstairs, had asked me to mind her cat for a weekend. His name was Stanislaus. Isn't that a terrible name for a cat? Mrs. Brigham called him Stan for short. Anyway, I said I'd be glad to mind Stan so off she went. Well, I had only seen the cat once or twice, slinking down the hall or disappearing like a shadow into the sitting room. So all I knew about him was that Mrs. Brigham bragged he was a purebred tortoiseshell with pedigree papers and he was worth a fortune."

The foam on Mrs. Flowers' soda went flat from stirring. "It was almost dark, that first night, when I discovered Stan was missing. So I sent Roger out the back and I went out the front calling, 'Here, Kitty, Kitty,' in my sweetest, wheedly voice. Then I heard meowing halfway up the soft maple on the lawn. When he saw me that rascal scrambled even higher. I coaxed and coaxed but he just wouldn't come down. Then Roger appeared with an open can of salmon. Roger was clever like that; he could always come up with an idea. He held the can high enough under the tree for the cat to get a whiff. And down came that prize tortoiseshell. Well, before he knew what was happening, I had him by the scruff. He snarled and clawed at me like a wildcat, but I managed to keep him at arm's length until I had him safe inside the house."

She burst out laughing. "I scolded that cat all the way down the hall into Mrs. Brigham's kitchen. Then, just before I dropped him, I happened to notice a snapshot on the windowsill that made me do a double take. It was a picture of a tortoiseshell cat with a black-striped nose. I looked at the cat that I held by the scruff. He looked exactly the same . . . except he didn't have a black stripe down his nose."

"Oh, no!" cried Janey. "You kidnapped the wrong cat!"

"That's right. You are looking at a real live cat-napper."

Norma laughed so hard she nearly fell off the stool. "Then what did you do?" she screeched.

"Well, I ran down the hall, still holding that ferocious cat at arm's length, and flung him out the door. When he was safely out of reach he turned around and gave me the cattiest glare you ever saw in your life."

Mr. White, who had been eavesdropping again, slapped the marble countertop and let out a loud guffaw. Janey and Norma were doubled over with laughter. "Did you ever find the real Stanislaus?" gasped Janey.

Mrs. Flowers bobbed her head gleefully. "At that very moment who should come strutting up the front walk, proud as a lion, but Stanislaus himself. The impostor quickly skirted around him and scrambled back up the tree."

"Oh, that's a wonderful story!" cried Janey, rubbing her stomach to relieve the laugh-cramps. "Would you mind if I used it for my next composition?"

"I'd be honoured," smiled Mrs. Flowers. "I think I'll tell it to my class tomorrow, too." She hopped off the stool, pulled on her hat and gloves, snapped the tail back into the fox's mouth and picked up her briefcase. "Well, I must be on my way. It was nice meeting you, Norma. And I'll see you Sunday, Jane. Goodbye now!"

Janey stared after Mrs. Flowers until the last trill of the doorbell had faded away. "See you Sunday?" she repeated with a puzzled frown.

"What's happening on Sunday?" Norma's green eyes were sparkling like emeralds.

"I don't know. C'mon, Norma, let's go."

On their way up Wheeler Street Janey was quiet, but Norma was talking a blue streak. "I think Mrs. Flowers is really nice, Janey. And she's pretty, too. And she's so much fun. My mother never tells swell stories like that. I like Mrs. Flowers, don't you, Janey?"

Janey stopped and didn't speak for a minute. Then she said, "I think I love her, Norma. But don't forget your promise not to say a word."

"Don't worry. I won't. Oh my gosh, there's Lester-de-pester playing right in the middle of the road again!" Norma put on a burst of speed and ran to rescue her little brother.

As she neared the purple house, Janey's footsteps slowed. Had Daddy invited Mrs. Flowers for supper again? If he had, what did it mean? That she really was his lady-friend? Her dad seemed much happier since he'd met Elinor. And she was such a nice lady. Just thinking about her made Janey smile. She knew that Mike and Patty liked her, too. But what about Amy?

She hoped her dad had told Amy whatever it was that was going to happen on Sunday. Because *she* didn't want to be the one to bring it up.

Chapter 21

Mrs. Flowers' Flat

By the end of the week her dad hadn't said a word, and Amy had gotten over her bad mood. Janey hated to spoil it by asking her if she knew what was happening on Sunday.

Saturday night her Dad came out of his den, all gussied up as usual. He stood in the kitchen doorway smoothing the brim of his fedora. "By the way, Vinny," he said coaxingly, "we're all invited to Mrs. Flowers' flat for dinner tomorrow. So you won't need to bother your head about Sunday supper."

Amy was writing a letter to Harry. She dipped the pen-nib into the bottle of ink and wrote a few more words. Then, without raising her head, she said, "Mrs. Plum has invited me to their house for Sunday supper."

Janey glanced from one to the other and saw the same stubborn expression on both faces. "Maybe you could go to Winnie's *next* Sunday, Amy," she suggested.

Before Amy had a chance to reply, her dad said, "Good idea, Petty. That solves the problem nicely. Well, I'll be away, then. Don't wait up."

᰾ ᰾ ᰾

Sharp at three o'clock Sunday afternoon John Phair came out of his den all dandied up again and smacked his palms together. "Let's get a move on!" he shouted.

Janey and the boys were ready and waiting. "Do you think it would be all right if I brought Purry-Motor, Daddy?" The marmalade cat was reclining upside down in her arms, purring as usual.

"Sure, Petty. Why not? Elinor's quite taken with the creature." With his hand on the newel post he glanced up the stairway. "Where's your sister? Isn't she ready?"

"She's not coming, Daddy." She rearranged the cat in her arms. "She's decided to go to Winnie's instead."

Her father stomped his foot on the bottom step, then changed his mind, turned on his heel and marched out the door.

Black Beauty was waiting by the curb. "Does she need a cranking, Dad?" asked Patty.

"No. She's all warmed up and raring to go."

The boys hopped in the back seat and Janey slid in beside her father. Without a backward glance he stepped on the gas and the Durante sedan went leap-frogging down Wheeler Street.

Mrs. Flowers was leaning out the window above the Red Rose Cafe on Gerrard Street, a long string of beads swinging from her neck.

"Yoo-hoo!" she cried, waving a tea towel like a welcome flag.

"Yoo-hoo!" returned Janey, waving her best handkerchief right back.

They scrambled out of the car and followed their dad up a long flight of stairs beside the cafe.

Mrs. Flowers stood, smiling, at the top. "Welcome to my house," she beamed and Janey thought how stylish she looked in her fringed flapper dress and spiked heels and silk net stockings.

Then her mouth fell open in surprise as Mrs. Flowers threw her arms around her father's neck and planted a loud smacker on his cheek. Then, swooping Purry-Motor from Janey's arms, she led the way in.

It wasn't really a house, it was three rooms in a row leading off a long hallway. Janey had never been in a flat before and she found it fascinating.

The first door was slightly ajar and she caught

a glimpse of a frilly bed and curtains. "That's my boudoir," smiled Mrs. Flowers. "I call it that just for fun." The next door was wide open. "And this is my sitting room. Go right in and make yourselves at home."

The little sitting room was stuffed with furniture: a velour chesterfield piled high with coloured cushions; an easy chair and matching ottoman; a gramophone and radio and floor lamp, and an end-table with a candlestick telephone sitting on a doily. All this furniture was crowded onto a floral Wilton carpet. Janey gazed around in wonder.

Mike and Pat made a beeline for the sofa, but they couldn't find anywhere to sit.

"Just throw the cushions on the floor and make room for yourselves," laughed Mrs. flowers.

Their father went straight to the easy chair, put his feet up on the ottoman, and made himself comfortable. Just as naturally, Janey thought, as if he were at home.

"How would you boys like to see my pictures?" Mrs. Flowers handed them a wooden stereoscope and a box of double photographs. "They're three-dimensional." She pulled the chain on the floor lamp and a rosy glow shone through the red silk shade onto the sofa. "They're scenes of the prairies and the Rocky Mountains. I tinted them myself with watercolours. I'm quite proud of them, if I do say so myself."

"Oh, Mrs. Flowers!" Janey cried. "Have you been out west?"

"Yes, indeed. My husband worked in Vancouver before the war," she explained.

In her mind's eye, Janey saw the golden wheat fields and blue skies of the prairies. A wave of homesickness washed over her.

"Where's your sister?" Mrs. Flowers' sudden question interrupted Janey's thoughts.

"She didn't want to come," piped up Patty.

"She was already invited to Winnie's," explained Janey.

"Well, maybe next time," said Mrs. Flowers. Then Purry began squirming in her arms. She set him down and off he went, exploring.

"How would you like to give me a hand in the kitchen, Jane?" Janey had noticed that Mrs. Flowers always called her by her proper name. She liked it. It made her feel grown-up.

"Okey-doke!" she said, and followed Mrs. Flowers to the bright little room at the end of the hall. "Amy hardly ever lets me help," she confided. "She always says 'you stick to your books.'"

Elinor nodded and handed her a stack of plates decorated with bluebells. "Well, I'm sure she means well," she said. "Your education should come first."

As they worked, they chatted happily together. Almost like mother and daughter, Janey thought.

When everything was ready Elinor called, "Soup's on!" But soup was just the beginning: then came crackling ham and crispy fries and creamy peas and carrots. And for dessert . . . ambrosia with pink cherry pound cake!

Janey couldn't help but notice how happy they all were, crowded around Elinor's little kitchen table. Especially her father. If only Amy were here to see, she thought.

After supper Janey helped carry the dishes to the sink. "I'll do them later," Mrs. Flowers said. "I don't want to waste a precious moment of your visit."

"Oh, Elinor!" In her excitement Janey forgot the Mrs. "You sound just like my Papa . . . I mean my Uncle Wallace. Only he sings the words like this: 'Leave the dishes in the sink, love, leave the dishes in the sink; each dirty plate will have to wait, tonight we're going to celebrate . . . so leave the dishes in the sink'!"

"I love it!" cried Elinor Flowers, clapping her hands. "Come on, everybody, let's have a party!" Spreading her arms like wings she swept them all back into the sitting room.

Lifting the lid of the gramophone, she put on a record, wound the handle on the side, and carefully lowered the needle-arm. Out of the speaker came a velvet voice crooning, "Cuddle up a little closer, lovey mine . . . " Elinor turned to Janey's father. "Johnny, let's dance!" she said.

Johnny! Janey had never heard her father called that before. It made him sound so young and debonair! Leaping to his feet, he held out his arms. With a sparkling smile, Elinor went into his arms as if she belonged there.

Janey watched them, starry-eyed, as they twirled around the tiny sitting room. "I didn't know you were a dancer, Dad!" she cried, clapping her hands to the music.

"Hah!" He dipped Elinor backwards, almost touching Janey's knees, and laughed out loud. "You should have seen me in my younger days, Petty. I could have danced all night." Then they spun out the door and down the length of the hall and back again.

When it was over the gramophone had slowed almost to a stop, so Michael put another record on and wound it up again. Out of the speaker came Eddie Cantor singing, "Baby face . . . you've got the cutest little baby face . . . " and Janey's father took her hands and pulled her to her feet. Janey was a good dancer. Her Uncle Wallace had taught her when she was so little she had to dance standing on his feet.

The next record Michael put on made John Phair burst into song: "Every morning, every evening, Ain't we got fun? Not much money, Oh but honey, Ain't we got fun?"

Michael laughed and said, "Wanna dance, Shortstop?"

So her father handed her over and took Elinor back again and the four of them twirled around the tiny room, laughing and bumping into each other.

Meantime, Patrick had parked himself on the windowsill with his drawing pad on his knee.

When the music stopped Janey looked over Patty's shoulder. He had captured every detail in charcoal: Elinor's long string of beads sailing out behind her; little Janey and tall Michael dancing like Mutt and Jeff; Purry-Motor perched on the sofa back with his fluffy tail curled around his feet. Only Amy was missing. If only she were here, Janey thought. She would love this.

"Oh, Daddy! Elinor!" Janey cried. "Come and see what Patty is doing.

Elinor took the drawing pad from Patty's hands and held it up to the light. "Why, it's wonderful,

Patrick," she marvelled. "You didn't tell me that your second son was an artist, John."

He peered over her shoulder and pursed his lips. It was the first time Janey had ever seen her father really look at one of Patty's drawings. "It is good," he conceded.

Patty flushed with pride.

Collapsing on the sofa among the cushions, Elinor said, "This is a storybook evening, Jane. Be sure you record it in your copybook. Someday you might want to write it in a real book."

Then she turned to Michael, who was sitting on the carpet, hugging his knees. "How about you, Michael? Have you got a special talent?"

Mike shrugged his shoulders. "I don't think so," he said.

"Yes you have, Mikey," Janey said. "You always get the highest marks in arithmetic."

"It's called Mathematics in high school, Shortstop," Michael corrected her.

"Perhaps you'll be an accountant, then; they make very good wages," said Elinor.

Now she turned to their father, who had loosened his necktie and was relaxing in the easy chair again. "What about Amy, John? What does your eldest want to do with her life?"

He frowned at the mention of Amy. "I suppose

she'll be content to be a housewife," he muttered. "That's all she really knows."

Janey gasped and jumped to her feet and wagged her finger in his face. "Oh, no, Daddy!" she cried. "Our Amy is a musician. Mrs. Plum says she could be a first-class pianist if she had more schooling."

Elinor's eyes widened with interest. "Who is Mrs. Plum?" she asked.

"She's Amy's best friend's mother. She says our Amy is gifted. Amy was playing the piano at their house one day — she plays by ear, you know — and Mrs. Plum discovered that she had perfect pitch. So she gave Amy free piano lessons and Amy won first prize at the Kew Beach Music Festival." Janey stopped talking because she had run out of air.

"Why, that's wonderful," Elinor said. "How far did Amy go in school, John?"

Janey saw another frown gathering on her father's forehead so she hurried on. "She finished third form high school. She got good marks, too. Then Gramma got very sick and Amy had to stay home to take care of her and keep house."

"Hmmm." Elinor tapped her lips thoughtfully. "Well . . . maybe now that that burden is lifted, Amy could make up for lost time. What do you think, John?"

Jumping out of the chair as if he'd been stung by a bee, he barked, "Come along you lot. It's time we were making tracks." Then he headed down the hall.

Mrs. Flowers hurried after him with a puzzled look on her face. "What's your rush, John?" she asked.

Instead of answering her, he addressed his family. "Tell Mrs. Flowers thank you for a fine evening," he ordered. They all thanked her very much.

Descending the dark staircase with Purry-Motor in her arms, Janey felt empty, like a deflated balloon. "This might turn into another dilemma, Purry," she whispered. He twitched his ears as if he understood.

Chapter 22

Missing Winnipeg

*I*n the weeks following their visit to Mrs. Flowers' flat, John Phair was in a morose mood. Still, practically every night he got dressed up and left the house. Michael and Patrick took full advantage of his absence.

Winter had set in almost overnight and a thick flurry of snow blew into the kitchen as the boys started out the back door.

"Where do you think you're off to?" demanded Amy.

"None of your beeswax," snapped Michael.

"Yeah, I second it," sauced Patrick.

"Well, it just so happens it is my business. When Gramma died Father put me in charge of this family." Amy tried to sound authoritative. "So you two get right back in here and finish your homework."

"Drop dead!" snorted Michael. "Yeah!" snickered

Patrick. They laughed and punched each other as they went out the door.

Janey was sitting at the table nervously chewing the eraser off the end of her pencil.

"Stop that nasty habit this instant and get to work on your lessons," Amy ordered. "At least one person in this family is going to get an education, or my name isn't Amy Lavinia Phair."

Slumping down on the chair opposite Janey she ran her fingers through her dishevelled hair. "*I* couldn't go to school like Mike and Patty. Oh, no!" Amy was ranting now, making Janey so nervous that she bit the eraser into bits and pieces and spat it onto her books. "Every time there was a family crisis *I* had to stay home." Amy twisted a strand of hair round and round her finger. "Like the time Harry nearly died. And whenever Gramma had a bad spell. And the time Father got drunk and broke his head wide open. Anything! Everything! Gramma would say, 'Amy, you have to stay home.' Well, you *never* have to stay home, Jane Elizabeth. So you have no excuse not to stand at the top of your class."

Suddenly Janey slapped her book shut and picked a bit of pink rubber off the end of her tongue. "But I am not like you, Amy Lavinia," she said.

Amy glared at her. "What is that supposed to mean?"

"It means I don't care where I stand, just so long as I pass."

Amy's hand shot across the table and gripped Janey's wrist. "You *have* to care, Janey. Otherwise I've failed. Don't you understand?"

Wrenching her arm away, Janey rubbed her stinging wrist. "Aunt Bessie always said the most important thing is to be happy," she said.

Groaning in frustration, Amy scraped back her chair and stumbled out of the room.

Janey heaved a big sigh. Talking about Aunt Bessie made her think of Winnipeg. "I wonder what Harry's doing right now?" she thought. The moon-faced clock on the wall said eight. "That means it's six o'clock in Winnipeg," she said to Purry who was curled up on her lap. "Suppertime. Pearl Mead probably left something good in the oven. Shepherd's pie, maybe."

She could picture the Vine Cottage kitchen as plain as day. It would be very cold in Winnipeg, colder than Toronto. Papa Wallace would put an extra log in the stove and poke at it until red sparks flew in the air. Then he'd sit down with Harry and say, "How was your day, Henry?"

The thought of the crackling fire in the woodstove of the Vine Cottage made the purple house seem colder than usual, even though her dad had stoked up the coal furnace before he left.

She got up to put the kettle on and Purry jumped off her lap. Sliding open the curved lid of the wooden breadbox, she got out a fresh loaf and cut off the heel. She looked in the ice-box for butter, then remembered that her dad didn't buy ice in winter. The butter would be hard as a brick in the milk-box outside the back door. When the kettle boiled she made herself a cup of hot Postum. Then she sat back down at the table and Purry jumped up on her lap again. She dipped the crust in the Postum. It tasted good even without butter.

When she was finished her snack she packed all her books into her schoolbag, except her copybook which she opened to the last story: "Party Time at Mrs. Flowers' Flat." She turned the page and started a new story: "The Vine Cottage Kitchen."

Lost in her story, she didn't hear Amy until it was too late to shut the copybook. She expected Amy to start ranting about wasting time. But instead Amy spoke in a tired whisper. "I'm sorry, Janey. Can you ever forgive me?"

"Oh, Amy!" Janey jumped up and threw her arms around her sister. "It's not your fault. I'll try harder to be more like you. And Daddy should be here to see to those bad boys."

Amy smoothed the long curls behind Janey's ears. "No, don't be like me. You just stay as sweet as you are. I'm going to bed now, but you can stay up and finish your story. Leave the light on for the boys. Goodnight, dear."

"Goodnight, Amy."

Amy's footsteps paused in the parlour and the piano lid clicked open. Then the soft notes of "I Dream of Jeanie with the Light Brown Hair" came floating through the chilly air.

Janey finished her story and gave it a happy ending.

Chapter 23

The Workmen

*T*he next day, Janey and Norma-Jean were standing in front of Norma's house after school, talking, when Janey happened to glance up the street. A slat-sided truck was parked in front of the purple house. Janey said goodbye to Norma and ran the rest of the way home.

Two men in paint-streaked caps and coveralls were standing on the veranda talking to Amy. The older man was pointing to the sign on the truck door: *Bill Bunch and Son, Decorators.*

"We're here to paint your house," he explained.

"We don't want our house painted," Amy said.

"No!" Janey bounded up the steps. "We like it purple."

"It's not the outside I'm talking about, Missy," Mr. Bunch explained. "A Mr. John Phair hired us to paint and wallpaper the inside of the house. Here's the work order, signed and sealed." He handed Amy a sheet of yellow paper.

Looking past Amy's elbow, Janey said, "That's Daddy's signature all right."

Amy nodded and held the door open to let them in.

Bill Junior lugged in gallons of paint and armloads of wallpaper. His father set up a board the size of a door on two wooden horses. Then they set right to work.

Amy and Janey went into the kitchen to eat their lunch and discuss what was happening.

"I wonder why Daddy has decided to fix up the house all of a sudden?" puzzled Janey.

"I wonder, too," murmured Amy, pumping water into the dishpan. Then she looked out the window over the sink and said, "There's Norma on the porch with her little brother. You'd better be back off to school."

Janey was tucking her long brown curls under her blueberry tam when young Billy Bunch appeared at the parlour door holding a big oval frame in his hands. "I found this here picture in back of a closet," he said. "What do you want me to do with it?"

Janey's heart leapt into her throat. "Oh, Amy!" she cried. "It's Mama's picture. I knew Daddy wouldn't throw it out."

They held the picture between them, not saying a word. Then Norma-Jean pounded on the window. "Hurry up, Janey," she yelled. "It's freezing out here and Lester-de-pester is crying."

"What shall we do with it, Amy?" Janey asked.

"We'll decide later. You go to school now before Lester catches his death of cold."

ì&   ì&   ì&

That night, the minute her father stepped in the door and before he even got his coat off, Janey pulled him over to the dining-room table where the picture was lying face up. "The workmen found it in your closet, Daddy. What do you want us to do with it?"

He didn't touch the picture, just looked at it. His voice was ragged when he spoke. "That's for you and your sister to decide," he said. "Perhaps you'd like to hang it in your room."

"Oh, that's a good idea. Thank you, Daddy!" Hugging the picture to her chest, Janey raced up the stairs where Amy was lying down with another headache. "Amy! Amy!" she cried. "Daddy says we can hang Mama's picture wherever we like — even in our room!"

Amy's grey eyes opened in two slits like a cat's. "If it's up to us," she said, "then we'll hang it where it belongs: over the piano."

Janey leaned the frame away from her body and looked into her mother's violet-blue eyes, so like her own. "That might not be a good idea," she said.

Amy stood, took the picture from her sister, and went down the stairs. Janey followed her.

A painting of the Rockies hung over the piano. "Take it down," ordered Amy.

Janey climbed up on the piano stool, lifted the heavy picture off the wall, and laid it flat on top of the piano. Amy handed up the oval frame. Grunting from its weight, Janey managed to fit the wire on the back of the picture over the nail. "How's that?" she asked breathlessly.

Amy cocked her head. "A little to the left," she said. Janey moved it to the left. Then Amy smiled. "That's perfect," she said.

Just then their father came out of his den. His dark eyes flashed from the picture to Amy. "What are you up to?" he growled.

"You . . . you said we could decide, Daddy," Janey reminded him. But he kept his eyes glued on her sister.

Suddenly Amy began waving her hands wildly around the room at all the fresh paint and wallpaper and cried, "What are *you* up to, Father?"

His face flushed red and his bottom lip quivered with anger. "What I do is none of your business," he snarled. "I answer to no one." Then he spun on his heel, grabbed his coat and hat off the rack, and stormed out the door.

"Now do you see what I mean?" demanded Amy.

"Yyy . . . es." Janey knew exactly what Amy meant. The new car and the freshened house was not for their benefit. It was for Elinor Flowers, and Janey was secretly glad.

❧ ❧ ❧

By the end of the week the workmen were finished and the house was transformed.

Standing in the middle of the worn carpet, John Phair did a slow turn. "We're going to need a new davenport," he said.

"Oh, no, Daddy, not another davenport." Janey wrinkled her nose at the cracked old leather couch. "Davenports are old-fashioned. Can't we get a velour chesterfield and coloured cushions and an easy chair, like in Mrs. Flowers' flat?"

"Well, now, that's a fine idea, Petty. What do you say, Vinny?"

Janey eyed her sister anxiously. What would Amy say next?

"If you really want my opinion," Amy said. "What we really need is a new washer and new linoleum and new oilcloth for the kitchen table."

"Well, I think we need *everything*," Janey piped

up. "Can we afford everything, Daddy?"

"Hmmm." He slipped two fingers into his vest pocket and produced something they had never seen before: a bank book. He opened it and tapped his finger on the column of figures. "Maybe we can," he said. "I saw in the newspaper that Eaton's is having a big sale on Saturday. How would it suit you girls if the three of us went downtown and picked things out?"

Before Janey had a chance to answer, Amy said, "I promised Winnie I'd go with her to the Beaches show on Saturday."

Then Janey piped up again, "Well, maybe Mrs. Flowers can help us pick things out, Daddy."

Suddenly Amy threw up her hands and shrieked in their faces: "Mrs. Flowers, Mrs. Flowers, Mrs. Flowers!" Then she dashed up the stairs and slammed the bedroom door.

Janey looked at her father, expecting to see his face red with anger. But instead he just looked bewildered and left the house, shaking his head.

Chapter 24

More Surprises

"*I* don't know what I'm going to do, Norma," Janey confided in her best friend as they slogged through the snow to school. "Amy won't go with Daddy and me to pick out new furniture, but she nearly had a fit when I suggested Mrs. Flowers might help us. I don't know what to do!"

They had to stop at the curb to let the Ritchie's Dairy wagon rattle by. Icicles hung from the horse's whiskers and steam puffed out of his nostrils like smoke from little chimneys.

Norma drew in her head like a turtle and burrowed her nose in her scarf. It was the first day of December and the temperature had plunged overnight. "Maybe my mother could help," she mumbled through her muffler.

As they crossed the road Janey got a mental picture of the furniture in Norma-Jean's house. It was even worse than their own. "Thanks just the same, Norma," she said, "but I don't think Amy would like that either."

That night the whole family was in a cranky mood. Pat and Mike and Janey were all hunched over their books around the parlour table studying for their Christmas exams. Amy was supervising from the leather chair as she unpicked the collar of Michael's school shirt.

"I can't do this stuff," grumbled Patty, scratching his head with his pencil. "Why would an artist have to learn geometry anyhow?"

"For crying out loud, don't you know anything?" Mikey grunted in disgust. "An artist needs geometry to measure lines and angles and stuff. Geez!"

Janey was just about to add her two cents worth when the door blew open on a gust of wind and in came their father, his face beaming red.

"Where have you been, Daddy?" Janey scolded him. "We were worried about you. You should have phoned."

"Never you mind about me." His tone was playful as he hung up his coat. "And you might as well know, so you won't worry some more, that I'll be gone for a few days. Work at the plant is slow this time of year, so I thought I'd take me a holiday."

A holiday? Her dad never took holidays because

he didn't get paid for the days he didn't work. She darted a glance at Amy to see how she was taking this strange news.

Amy had turned the shirt collar back to front and was carefully pinning it in place. "Winter's an odd time for a holiday," she said without looking up.

"Well, it suits me to a T," retorted her father as he retreated into his den and closed the door.

Michael glared at the closed door and wrinkled his nose. "Something's fishy," he said.

"You're telling me," agreed Patrick.

"Maybe that's it," Janey said. "Maybe Daddy is going ice-fishing. Papa Wallace goes ice-fishing sometimes in the Red River. Anyway, that's my guess."

"Guess again, Shortstop," shot back Mikey.

"Well, then, I'm going to ask him because I want to know." She made a move to get up but Amy stopped her in her tracks.Pointing at the mantle clock with her needle, she snapped, "Sit down and finish your work. You've got another hour to put in."

≈ ≈ ≈

Their father was gone for three days and three nights. On the fourth day, early in the evening, when they were all buried in their books again, they heard a car backfiring out the front.

"That'll be him," Mikey said. "He's the only man

I know stubborn enough to drive in winter."

They all stopped what they were doing and stared at the front door. They heard Black Beauty's door clank shut and footsteps crackling on the icy veranda. Then the front door burst open in a shower of snow and in came their dad with Mrs. Flowers.

Janey jumped up to greet them but Amy grabbed her by the arm and jerked her back into her chair.

"I'm glad to see you're all here," their father said, and Janey heard an excited tremor in his voice, "because I have an important announcement to make." He put his arm around Mrs. Flowers and drew her closer to him. "Mrs. Flowers . . . Elinor and I . . ." He looked down into her sparkling eyes; her lashes were wet with snowflakes. "Well . . . the two of us . . . have eloped!"

Eloped? *Eloped!*

Janey's heart did somersaults. "Does that mean . . ." Oh, she hoped she was right! "Does that mean you got married, Daddy?"

"That's exactly what it means, Petty." He heaved a great sigh of relief as if he'd got a load off his chest.

"Oh, Daddy!" Janey gasped. "That's soooo romantic!" Breaking loose from Amy's grasp, she ran to them and nearly bowled them over.

Laughing with tears in her eyes, Mrs. Flowers

hugged Janey and gave her an Eskimo kiss with her cold nose.

Smiling from ear to ear, her father hung up his coat and hat. Janey thought he had never looked more handsome.

Elinor pulled off her snowy wool cloche and shook out her curly bobbed hair. Then she unsnapped her fox collar and her new husband helped her off with her coat.

The rest of the family sat as if mesmerized. Then Michael came to and strode over. "Congratulations, Dad," he said, and stuck out his hand. "You, too, Mrs. Flowers."

Patrick was right behind him. "I second it," he said. "But wouldn't it be Mrs. Phair now?"

Mrs. Phair! Janey thought her heart would burst with joy.

Elinor beamed and threw her arms around both boys. "That's right," she said. "I'm Mrs. Phair now. I'll have to get used to that, won't I?" Then she looked across the room at her eldest stepdaughter and the smile faded from her lips.

Amy's face was as pale as paper and her eyes were as cold and grey as slate. The room went suddenly quiet. The only sound that could be heard was the ticking of the clock.

Suddenly John Phair smacked his hands together, making everybody jump. "Vinny! Vinny!" Beseechingly, he held out his arms to Amy. "Come and welcome your new mother."

Oh, Daddy, Janey thought, I wish you hadn't said that. But it was too late. The words were out.

Amy had been knitting socks. Methodically, she wrapped the half-knit sock around the needles and put it her knitting bag. Then she got up, eyes straight ahead, and walked slowly towards the stairs.

"Vinny!" cried her father again.

Stopping on the bottom step, her hand clutching the newel post, she turned her head and looked at him. "Why don't you call *her* that, since she's taking my mother's place," she said.

Janey's heart turned over as she saw first pain, then anger, flash across her father's face. Then Elinor placed a hand on his arm and looked straight at Amy. "I am not here to take your mother's place, my dear," she said in a quiet voice. "But I am your father's wife, now, and I want you to respect me for that."

Bursting into tears, Amy stumbled up the stairs.

Janey started after her but her father held her back. "You stay here, Petty. This is my job," he said. He followed Amy up the stairs.

Elinor said, "Let's all go to the kitchen. I could use a cup of tea."

Some time later John Phair came back downstairs, dropped into his chair, and rested his head in his hands. Janey poured him a cup of tea and Elinor put her hand on his shoulder.

"Is she all right, Daddy?" Janey whispered.

"She'll be fine, Petty. Don't worry. She'll be fine." But he shook his head sadly. "Elinor wanted to have a proper wedding with all the family there. But I thought it best to elope in hopes of avoiding this scene. I guess I was wrong."

❧ ❧ ❧

When Janey crept into bed that night she knew Amy wasn't sleeping. And she knew she wasn't fine.

She lay still for a long time listening to the snow swooshing past the windowpane. Then she reached out and touched Amy's arm.

"Amy," she whispered. "Elinor told the boys and me that we could call her Mother if we liked, but we don't *have* to."

Amy pulled her arm away. "I will *never* call her mother," she answered bitterly. "I *had* a mother."

Janey thought that over and then she said, "But I didn't. I've never called anybody mother."

"Aunt Bessie was a mother to you," said Amy.

Janey thought that over, too. "No," she said. "She was my dearest aunt. But she was not my mother." Turning her head on the pillow until she could see Amy's still profile, she continued: "One of the last things Aunt Bessie ever said to me was . . . someday you might have another mother. I didn't understand what she meant then, but I do now."

There was no response from Amy so Janey turned on her side with Purry-Motor cuddled in her arms. "This is a terrible dilemma, Purry," she whispered and the cat purred softly as if he understood.

Chapter 25

Big Changes

*T*he very next day Mrs. Flowers' furniture arrived in a moving van. But, as Patty had pointed out, she wasn't Mrs. Flowers any more, she was Mrs. Phair now.

Mrs. Phair . . . Elinor Phair . . . Janey could hardly believe it. But for sure it was true because their marriage certificate hung in a beveled frame on the den wall where the oval picture used to be.

As the men trundled Elinor's furniture in the front door, her father and brothers lugged the old stuff out the back.

Then Mr. and Mrs. Phair arranged the furniture in a cosy circle on Elinor's Wilton carpet. Only the piano, and the picture above it, stayed in place.

"How does it look to you, Jane?" Elinor asked, her voice rippling with pleasure.

"Beautiful!" cried Janey. The velour chesterfield, coloured cushions, the end table with the candlestick telephone on the doily and the floor lamp with the red silk shade made the parlour of the purple house even prettier than the sitting room above the Red Rose Cafe.

Everything was in its place when Janey spied a corrugated carton, tied with dusty twine, sitting in a corner. "There's a box we forgot," Janey said. "I wonder what's in it?"

"Why don't you open it and see," Elinor suggested. "It might be something for you."

"For me?" Janey knelt and began pulling at the knot, but the more she pulled the tighter it got.

"Need some help, Shortstop?" Mikey snapped open his penknife and cut the twine with a twang.

It fell away in a puff of dust and Janey saw that there were words printed on the box. Brushing away the dust, she read: "Property of Roger W. Flowers." She looked up at Elinor.

"It belonged to my late husband. Go ahead and open it, Jane."

Four pieces of cardboard, tucked into each other, formed the top of the box. Janey pulled them apart and gasped at what she saw. "Why it's a . . . a typewriting machine!" she marvelled. "A Royal typewriting machine. But I don't know how to typewrite."

"Don't worry, I'll teach you," Elinor promised. "I taught Roger. He was a newspaper reporter before the war."

The wonderful machine made Janey forget everything else. "Amy!" she cried. "Amy! Come and see what I've got!"

Amy had stayed busy in the kitchen while all the moving was going on. Now she announced, "Supper's ready!" just as if she hadn't heard a thing.

John Phair sat in his usual place at the head of the table and Elinor was about to sit beside him when he said, "No, no, Sweetheart, you sit at the other end. That's your proper place now."

Sweetheart! What a sweetie Daddy is, Janey thought. Then she glanced around the table. The boys were grinning like Cheshire cats, but Amy was sitting stone-faced beside her. She realized then that Elinor had taken Amy's place at the foot of the table.

Amy had made beef stew and dumplings.

"This is the best dish I've ever tasted, Amy," Elinor said. "You'll have to give me your recipe." Amy didn't answer so Elinor persisted. "I hope you'll share all the family favourites with me."

"Mine is Scotch hash," Patrick piped up.

"Mine's corned beef and cabbage," Michael said.

"What's yours, Jane?" Elinor asked.

"I like everything Amy cooks," Janey said loyally.

"Well, this here beef stew and dumplings is my favourite," their father said and Amy almost smiled until he added, "And Elinor's chicken fricassee! Wait'll you taste it, Vinny. It's out of this world."

The rest of the meal passed in silence and as soon as they were finished eating the boys and their father hightailed it into the parlour, which had been renamed the sitting room.

Amy began noisily clearing the table.

Elinor rolled up her sleeves. "I'll help you, dear," she said.

"No, thank you." Amy shook a storm of soap flakes into the basin and added a gush of hot water from the kettle. "I prefer to work alone in *my* kitchen."

Two bright pink patches appeared on Elinor's cheeks. Rolling down her sleeves, she straightened her shoulders and walked quietly into the sitting room. Janey hesitated, then followed.

Mike and Patty had decided to stay in that Saturday night. "Is it all right if we play some records?" Michael asked his new stepmother.

"Of course." Elinor sat down beside her husband and Purry-Motor leapt into her lap.

Michael wound the gramophone and played records one after the other. All the while the music was playing Janey kept stealing glances at the newlyweds. In spite of everything she could tell that they were happy.

At the end of the song: "I want to be happy, but I can't be happy, till I make you happy, too!" Elinor's eyes strayed to the kitchen. "Let's ask Amy to play for us," she said. "There's nothing like live music."

"Good idea." Her husband leaned his head back and shouted. "Vinny! Come in here and play us a tune."

There was no answer from the kitchen. "She must be reading and didn't hear you, Daddy." Janey said. "I'll get her."

But Amy wasn't reading. A book was open on her lap but she was staring at the ceiling.

"Amy."

Her eyes blinked twice. "What?" she said.

"Daddy and Elinor and the boys and me . . . we want you to play something on the piano. Elinor says there's nothing like live . . . "

"I heard her."

"Well, will you?"

"Not tonight." Amy closed her book and straightened the new oilcloth on the table. "At least we've still got our own table," she muttered. "Have you finished your studies?"

"Yes."

"Then I want you to come to bed with me."

"But it's Saturday night, and I'm having fun."

As if she hadn't spoken, Amy took hold of Janey's hand and led her through the sitting room. "Say goodnight," she ordered.

"Goodnight, Daddy. Goodnight, Elinor." Salty tears were stinging Janey's eyes.

"Goodnight, Petty," answered her father.

"Goodnight my dears," said Elinor softly.

"Move over, Patty," said Amy.

He slid across the bottom step. He had been working on a picture all evening. It was a beautiful family portrait. And he had put Amy in it even though she wasn't there.

Janey turned to tell Elinor. But Elinor's head was sunk on her chest and her dark hair was hiding her face. Her husband was rubbing the back of her neck.

"Why are you stopping?" snapped Amy.

"I can't sleep without Purry-Motor," Janey pouted.

As if he understood, the marmalade cat jumped off Elinor's lap and followed them up the stairs.

Chapter 26

News from Winnipeg

DEar Harry:

I am writing to you on my nEw typE-writing machinE. It is a 'Royal' and I'll tEll you how I got it in a minutE. You will noticE thE small E's don't work so I havE to usE capital E's.

I know Daddy phonEd UnclE WallacE thE good nEws, but I want to tEll you all about it mysElf. I hardly know whErE to start so I'll bEgin at thE bEst part. Our nEw mothEr's namE is Elinor Flow-Ers . . . or it was until shE marriEd our dad. Now shE is Elinor Phair.

BEforE thEy got marriEd Daddy hirEd two mEn to paint and wallpapEr EvEry room in thE purplE housE. ThEn, whEn Elinor camE ShE brought all hEr prEtty furniturE from hEr flat on GErrard StrEEt. You would not rEcognizE thE housE now. It has bEEn transformEd. EvEn Daddy's dEn is spic-and-span.

I am writing with my pencil now because typewriting with two fingers is too slow. And it hurts my fingers because you have to bang the keys really hard so they will fly up and hit the paper. Also, I think I'll wait until Daddy gets the E fixed for me. He also said he would buy me typewriting and carbon paper so I can make copies of my stories. Then I'll send some to you.

Now I'll tell you about our new mother. She used to be a school teacher but now she is just a housewife because married women are not allowed to work. I don't know why. It doesn't seem fair to me.

Anyway, this is what happened: Daddy took holidays from work and he and Elinor ELOPED! (Which means they had a secret wedding). Isn't that romantic? Besides being romantic Elinor explained to me why they didn't have a proper wedding. First of all they have both been married before, Daddy to our mother, of course, and Elinor to a soldier named Roger who got killed in the Great War.

The other reason they eloped was because of Amy. Daddy said he was afraid she would throw a monkey wrench into their plans.

At first Amy refused even to speak to Elinor. Then Daddy had a serious talk to her and now she speaks when she is spoken to. But she never calls Elinor by name. And now that Elinor has taken charge of the house, Amy spends most of her free time at Winnie Plum's.

It is too bad Amy doesn't like Elinor because she is such a nice mother. And I've never seen Daddy so happy. He is transformed, just like the house. He does not yell or drink beer any more. Isn't that amazing?

How are the Pickles twins? I don't miss them any more but you can tell them Merry Christmas anyway. But do not say a word to Irma Pringle.

I have to go now, Harry, because I still have one more exam to study for before the Christmas holidays. That is one thing that has not changed. Amy still makes me study too hard.

Give my love to Uncle Wallace and Pearl Mead.

Your loving sister
Janey Phair.

P.S. Oh, yes, I promised to tell you how I got the typewriting machine. Well, you see, Elinor's old husband, Roger, used to be a newspaper reporter before he got killed in the war. So Elinor gave me his machine because she knows I want to be a writer, too, when I grow up.

J.E.P.

æ æ æ

"I would be the happiest girl in the world," Janey told Norma-Jean on the first day of the Christmas holidays, "if only Amy was happy, too."

Norma pulled a long stretch of gum out of her mouth and chewed it back in. "What does your stepmother say about Amy?" she asked.

"Don't call Elinor 'step,' Norma. She's just like a real mother to me."

"Then how come you don't call her mother?"

"Because Amy wouldn't like it. So Elinor said I could call her by her first name."

"Can I call her Elinor, too?"

"No! I don't call your mother Astrid, do I? I call her Mrs. Cox."

"Okey-doke, I'll call your new mother Mrs. Phair. What does Amy call her?"

Janey frowned. "She doesn't call her anything," she said. "Elinor says not to worry . . . give her time

. . . she'll come around. But I don't think she will.
Elinor doesn't know Amy like I do. Amy can be as
stubborn as Daddy when she wants to. Gramma
used to say they were both cut from the same cloth."

Just then Lester-de-pester poked his head out
the door of the Cox's house. "Norma-Jean! Mama
wants you!" he yelled.

Norma stuck her tongue out at him and said
goodbye to Janey.

The minute Janey walked in the kitchen door
Elinor said, "There's a letter for you from Winnipeg
on the table, Jane."

Janey shucked off her coat and ripped open the
letter.

> Winnipeg, Manitoba,
> December 20, 1931.

Dear Janey:
> We were all surprised here to get the news
> about the new stepmother. She sounds nice.
> But it don't make no difference to me because
> I am going to spend the rest of my born life
> here with Papa Wallace.

Harry is even beginning to *sound* like Papa,
Janey thought.

> He is learning me the woodworking trade.
> I especially like making coffins because peo-

ple want all kinds of interesting things carved on the lids. Like when little Percy Peebles died of pneumonia (he was only two years old), Mrs. Peebles ordered an angel carved on his lid. And when Barny Ballentine fell on the railway tracks and got hisself cut in half, Mrs. Ballentine wanted a devil carved on his lid because she said that's what killed him . . . devil-rum. But Papa said it would be bad luck to carve a devil and Pearl said it would be blashemouth . . . whatever that means.

Anyway, do you know what I found out about myself? That I am an artist, too, same as Patty. Only I make pictures on wood instead of paper. I carved leaves around the edge of old Mr. Pennyworth's coffin (he died of old age) and Papa Wallace said he couldn't have done better his own self. I'd like to quit school right now and be his helper. But he says I have to go all the way through high school. But I don't see why because he only went to the fourth grade hisself and look how good he done!

Pearl Mead says to tell you that she is real happy you got a nice new mother. She says, "Janey is a good girl and virtue is its own reward," whatever that means.

Well, I hope you have a Merry Christmas and Happy New Year. I think you will now you got a new mother (and new father, too, by the sounds of it).

I'm glad you got that typewriting machine, Janey. Typewriting will make your stories look more real. Especially if you get the E fixed.

Yours truly,
Harry Phair.

Elinor couldn't help but smile at Harry's letter. "He sounds like a bright young man," she said.

Just then Purry-Motor, who had been snoozing on the crest of the chesterfield, bounced in the air like an India rubber ball and landed smack in the middle of a box of Christmas decorations that lay open on the sitting room floor.

Clapping her hands, Elinor cried, "Get out of there, you rascal!" and he streaked away with tinsel streaming from his ears.

Janey's dad had put the tree up on a wooden stand the night before, and she and Elinor began to decorate it.

Elinor had brought her own decorations from her flat. "I love a pretty tree," she said, holding up a tinkling silver bell. Then she added softly, "This was Roger's favourite."

"I'll show you mine." Janey rummaged through the old box of decorations from the attic until she found what she was looking for . . . a hand-knit Santa Claus. "Aunt Bessie made it for me when I was a tiny little girl," she said. Then, from a cocoon of cotton batting, she held up a clear glass ball with a winter scene painted all around it. "My mother decorated this herself," she said. "Its Amy's favourite."

"Oh, it's exquisite," Elinor said. Then she asked, "By the way,where is Amy? She might like to help us dress the tree."

"She's at Winnie's," Janey said, carefully returning the glass ball to its white cocoon. "Amy likes to hang it up herself,"she explained.

It seems as if Amy is always over at Winnie's these days, Janey thought. And her dad was on the night shift at the plant again, and Mikey and Patty were out "running the roads like a loose Ford wheel'" as her gramma used to say, so Janey had her new mother all to herself.

Chapter 27

Happy Holidays?

*T*he tree was the most beautiful Janey had ever seen. The pink light from the red silk lamp sparkled in the glass balls and glistened on the icicles and reflected like stars in Janey's shining eyes.

"Where's Amy?" her dad said. "She should be home on Christmas Eve." "She's over at Winnie's. I'll phone her and tell her to come home."

"You do that, Petty," he said.

But just as she was about to dial the Plums' phone number, they heard Amy open the kitchen door.

"Come in here, Vinny!" her father called. Amy came into the sitting room with her coat still on. "Isn't that a sight to behold?" he said, waving his hand at the tree.

Janey held her breath. Surely Amy would admire the tree. She breathed a sigh of relief when

Amy replied, "It's very pretty, Father."

"Well, off with your coat, then, and let's have a Christmas carol."

Amy had not played the piano since Elinor's arrival. But Janey knew, because Winnie had told her, that Amy often played at the Plums' house.

Amy hung up her coat and hat and sat down at the piano. She lifted the lid and ran her fingertips along the keys. Janey opened the book of carols at "Silent Night."

Then the whole family gathered around as she began to play. They sang all the old familiar carols and, before they knew, it two hours had passed by like magic.

"You play beautifully, my dear," Elinor said.

"Thank you," Amy answered. She rose from the piano bench and went straight up the stairs.

"Let's have a snack," Mikey said. "I'm starved."

"Me too!" echoed Patty.

Elinor made hot chocolate and Janey set a green glass plate full of shortbread and mince tarts on the table. When the hot chocolate was steaming in their cups Elinor said, "Perhaps Amy would fancy something."

But Janey said, "No, I think she's tired now."

And her father nodded his head in agreement.

❧ ❧ ❧

"Christmas was amazing this year, Norma," Janey said, as she held up her arms and spun around to show off her new outfit.

"I like your new coat and tam," complimented Norma. Cracking the tip off a candy cane with her big front teeth she handed the rest of it to Lester.

"It's not a tam, Norma, it's a French beret! Elinor bought both me and Amy a new coat and French beret!"

"So . . . does that mean Amy had an amazing Christmas, too?"

"You're nosy, Norma-Jean," laughed Janey.

"I know . . . but did she?"

"I think she did." Janey took her mitten off and leaned down to make a hand print in a fresh snowdrift. "Her new coat is exactly like Winnie Plum's and she almost smiled when she opened it."

"Well, that's a good sign." They stopped to pat Barney, the Canada Bread man's horse. He nickered and slobbered on Norma's new angora muff. "My dad gave my mother a new toaster that turns the bread over automatically!" she boasted.

"Well, *my* dad gave Elinor a diamond ring!" bragged Janey.

Norma-Jean's eyes grew as big as silver dollars. "A *real* diamond ring?"

"Well, no, but he said it *would* be real someday."

Janey tucked a stray curl under her beret. "And you know what else, Norma?"

"What?"

"Patty painted Elinor a beautiful flower picture and Mikey made a frame for it and Daddy hung it up over the piano."

"Over the piano!" Norma stopped dead in her tracks. "What happened to your mother's portrait?"

"Well . . . Amy didn't mind *too* much since it was Patty's painting. She asked Daddy to hang Mama's picture in our bedroom."

"Oh, that's nice," Norma sighed. "We had chicken for Christmas dinner, what did you have?"

"We had goose and Elinor stuffed and cooked it and Amy even helped her. Oh, it was lovely. Everything was lovely."

ঌ ঌ ঌ

But the warm glow of Christmas only lasted until New Year's. The next day their dad went back to work, Janey and the boys went back to school and Elinor took the tree down. And when the tree went out the door, all the happiness seemed to go out with it.

At noon hour Janey came home to find Elinor and Amy quarreling in the kitchen.

"Leave me alone!" wailed Amy. Then she grabbed her old coat off the cellar door and went slamming out of the house.

Elinor stared at the door, her eyes filling with tears. "I thought everything was going to be all right after such a lovely Christmas," she moaned. "But no, she's as impossible as ever. She won't even wear her new coat. It's still in the box. What *does* she want? What *would* make that girl happy?"

For the rest of the day Janey worried. What *does* Amy want? What *would* make her happy? Then suddenly it came to her, like a light bulb flashing on.

Racing home from school, she flew in the kitchen door all out of breath. "Elinor! Elinor!" she cried. "I think I've got it!"

Elinor came running down the stairs. "Got what? What have you got?"

Janey had to gulp down a big breath of air before she could say it. "I think I know what she wants," she gasped.

"You do?" Elinor's voice rose hopefully as she helped Janey off with her coat. "Well, for heaven's sakes, tell me. I'll try anything at this point. I'm at my wit's end."

Janey pulled off her beret and shook out her chestnut curls. "She wants to go back to school," she said breathlessly. "She wants to finish her education. But she thinks it's too late now because she's missed two years."

"To school?" Elinor's eyes sparked with excitement. "But it's not too late. Why, she's only seventeen. I'm sure I could help her make up those two years . . . if she'd only let me. I *am* a teacher, after all, and a smart girl like Amy would catch up very quickly with proper tutoring."

Suddenly Janey had misgivings. "What if Daddy says no?" she worried. "It was him who made her quit school in the first place."

"Well, I'm here now." Elinor set her mouth in a determined line. "And as the woman of this house, it's about time I took a stand." Marching into the sitting room, she picked up the candlestick phone. "What is Mrs. Plum's phone number?"

"It's Grover 492. Why do you want to talk to Mrs. Plum?"

"I don't. I want to talk to your sister."

She dialed the number. "Hello, Mrs. Plum? This is Mrs. Phair. Is Amy there? No, I don't wish to speak to her. Would you please send her home? Thank you. Goodbye." She hung up.

Chapter 28

Partners

Amy came rushing in the kitchen door all out of breath. "What's the matter?" she cried. "What's happened?"

"Nothing's the matter," Elinor said. "I'm sorry if I frightened you. Take off your coat and sit down."

Amy and Janey sat opposite each other at the kitchen table. Elinor sat between them, in their father's chair. Clasping her hands in front of her, she looked at Amy and said, "Jane has just told me that you'd like to go back to school."

Amy huffed in exasperation. "Why would you say that, Janey? You know I've missed two years. Winnie is in fourth form already. I'd even be behind Mikey."

"But Amy . . . Elinor says she can help you catch up."

Amy shook her head doubtfully, so Elinor continued, "I wasn't a schoolteacher all those years for nothing, Amy. And it's only January. If we both work very hard I'm sure I could catch you up to Winnie between now and next fall."

Amy was speechless, so Janey blurted out, "Oh, Amy, you're the smartest person I know. And if you work as hard as you make me work I'm sure you could do it."

Amy almost smiled at that, then she said, "What about father? What did he say?"

"Well . . . " Janey frowned. "We haven't asked *him* yet."

"And what if he says no?"

Elinor patted both their hands. "You just leave him to me," she said. "I can be very persuasive when I want to."

"She can, Amy. She really can!" cried Janey. "Just look at all the changes she's made since she became our moth . . . our friend." Jumping up to the sink Janey turned on the faucet and sparkling water spurted out of the tap. "Remember how badly Gramma wanted rid of that old sink-pump? And we've got a new Coldspot that holds a hundred pounds of ice. And a Thor washing machine that you just have to plug in the wall . . . and . . . "

"Shhh!" whispered Amy. Then she said, as if thinking out loud, "Winnie will be going to Normal

School in the fall to become a teacher . . . I only wish . . . "

"What do you wish?" prompted Elinor.

"I wish I could go with her."

"Then you shall, Amy, you shall." Elinor jumped up and got her recipe box down from the shelf above the stove. She had brought it with her from her flat and she made wonderful new dishes out of it. "What's that old saying about the way to a man's heart?" She smiled as she riffled through the recipe cards.

"Oh, I know that one," giggled Janey. "'The way to a man's heart is through his stomach.' That's what Pearl Mead always says."

Elinor laughed. "And I'll bet she says 'many hands make light labour' too."

"Yes, she does. How did you know that?"

With a sly wink Elinor handed Janey her pinafore and Amy her apron.

Together they made a supper fit for a king.

ða ða ða

When the table was cleared and the boys had gone out, John Phair sat contentedly patting his stomach and sipping his tea. Then he realized that three pairs of eyes were fastened on him.

"What is it? What are you all looking at?" He pulled in his chin and looked down his front to see if he'd slopped on his shirt.

"Jane." Elinor nodded her head. "Tell your father what you told me. Let's get his opinion."

Janey glanced at Amy, who was studying the tea leaves in the bottom of her cup.

"Well, Petty . . . " Her father wiped his mouth on his napkin and he didn't belch the way he used to. "I'm listening. What have you got to say for yourself?"

She wanted to say, for the hundredth, millionth time, "Don't call me Petty any more," but she figured that could wait. Reaching out impulsively, she clutched his hand. The coarse black hairs on his knuckles scratched her palm. She took a deep breath and blurted it all out in one sentence. "Our Amy wants to go back to school and become a teacher like Winnie Plum and Elinor is going to help catch her up aren't you Elinor?"

Elinor nodded her head yes.

John Phair's eyebrows bunched over his straight nose like a black caterpillar. His sharp eyes darted from daughter to daughter, then settled on his wife. "Is it possible?" he asked. "She's fallen years behind."

"Sure it's possible, Daddy!" Janey jumped in before Elinor had time to open her mouth. "Amy is the smartest in our family. And she's got lots of music credits. Mrs. Plum says all she needs is her high school diploma. Then she can go to Normal School and be a music teacher."

He began stirring his tea. He stirred so long that Janey was just about to burst out talking again when her father reached over and raised Amy's chin with his finger. "Is this what you want, Vinny?" he asked.

Amy slowly raised her eyelashes and met his earnest gaze. "Yes, Father, it is what I want. And I'm not so far behind as you might think. You see, Winnie has been tutoring me since September."

Janey and Elinor's eyes met. So that was why Amy had been spending so much time at the Plums' lately. Maybe it hadn't been completely Elinor's fault after all.

"I told you it was possible, Daddy!" cried Janey.

"That's a big word . . . possible." He dragged his fingers down his face in that way he had when he was wrestling with a problem.

"What is it, Johnny?" whispered Elinor.

"Even if she qualifies, I'm not sure I can afford it. Michael is not through school yet. And you seem to think Patrick should go on to Art College. Think of the expense! It's all I can do to put food on the table and keep a roof over our heads. I'm lucky to have a job in these hard times."

Janey's blue eyes darted anxiously from one to the other. Then Elinor spoke again. "Johnny," she said, *"We* can afford it."

It took a second for her meaning to sink in. Then he exploded. "Oh, no!" He thumped his fist on the table. "Not on your life. I'll not take money from a woman."

Elinor jumped up so suddenly her chair went over with a crash. Startled, they stared at her and saw, for the first time, anger flashing in her eyes.

She picked up the chair. "I am deeply disappointed in you, John Phair," she said, her voice frosty. "I thought when we women got the vote, back in 1920, that we were finally equals with men. So I assumed, when I married you, that we would be partners. But it seems I was wrong."

Shoving the chair in against the table with a loud crack, she marched through the sitting room and into the den and slammed the door.

John Phair's face was the picture of bewilderment.

"Oh, Daddy!" Janey wagged her finger in his face. "Now see what you've done." Then she jumped up, shoved her chair in with a crack, and followed her stepmother.

Elinor was sitting on the bed nuzzling Purry-Motor. She patted the eiderdown and Janey sat beside her. "Let's leave them alone a minute," Elinor whispered between the cat's ears. Like two girls in a conspiracy, they linked arms and crossed fingers and held their breath and waited.

They didn't have long to wait. About two minutes later there came a tapping on the door.

"Yes . . . who is it?" called Elinor sweetly.

The answer came in a subdued male voice: "It's me, your partner."

Springing off the bed Janey flung open the door. "You can come in now, Daddy!" she cried.

"And you can go out now, Petty," he replied, gently pushing her through the door.

Chapter 29

Conspirators

*T*he months sped by like a roller-coaster. Amy was so busy with her own studies that she forgot all about Janey's.

"And you know what, Norma?" Janey flung her beret into the air and ran to catch it. "I'm doing even better than when Amy was nagging me all the time."

"Do you want to come to my house for supper tonight, Janey? So it will be quiet in your house for Amy to study?"

"Will Lester-de-pester be there?"

"Of course, he's my brother."

"Well, what's your mother making for dessert?" Janey tucked her hair under her beret.

"She always makes Lardy Cake on Fridays. It's Lester-de-pester's favourite."

Janey tried not to make a face. Mrs. Cox's Lardy

Cake was even worse than the stale-bread pudding Gramma used to make.

"How about you come to my house, Norma. Amy always studies with Winnie on Friday nights. Elinor said she was going to make Lazy Daisy cake because she knows it's my favourite."

"Oh, I love Lazy Daisy. Will she mind if I come?"

"Of course not. She says you're always welcome."

"She's nice," Norma said.

"I know," agreed Janey.

By the end of June Amy Phair had caught up with her peers and passed her finals with flying colours. Janey's heart nearly burst with pride when she saw her sister walk across the high school stage to receive her diploma.

All sorts of wonderful things happened that summer. Amy got her hair shingled into a wind-blown bob like Elinor's, and her headaches seemed to magically disappear. Janey got her very first undergarment that was not a shirt or bloomers (it was called a brassiere, but not out loud) and Harry came home for his holidays. He had grown two inches taller than Janey and had lost all of his baby ways. Janey was proud as punch of him.

Aunt Celia and Uncle Donald and their family came down from Orillia, and Uncle Bill Phair and his second wife, Aunt Moira, came all the way from Ottawa in his Hudson car to meet Elinor.

At the family picnic in Kew Beach Park, Janey over heard her uncle say to her dad, "You're looking grand, John. Married life seems to agree with you. You're a lucky man. Your new wife's a knockout."

Her dad's chest swelled up like a rooster and he almost choked on his pride. "It would take a bigger word than 'knockout' to describe my Elinor," he crowed. Janey had never been happier.

⁂

On the first day of August, Janey and Norma-Jean sat on the back porch of the purple house excitedly poring over the new Eaton's Fall and Winter Catalogue. Elinor had ordered a new breadbox (to her horror, she had discovered maggots in the old wooden one), and the Eaton driver, with his horse, Sandy, had delivered the catalogue along with the order.

Janey glanced up to see Amy talking to the postman on the front sidewalk. Amy signed a piece of paper and the postman handed her a letter. Then she hurried up the walk.

"Hi, Amy!" Norma liked Amy.

"Hello, Norma."

"Mrs. Phair invited me for supper again."

Amy stopped on the top step. "I'm sorry, Norma,

but you can't stay today. Maybe tomorrow."

"That's not fair, Amy," Janey complained. "She's already invited."

"Is father home yet, Janey?"

"No. It's only five o'clock. Why can't Norma-Jean stay?"

Amy went indoors as if she hadn't heard the question.

Norma jumped up, her freckled face turning red. "I'm mad!" she cried and stomped off home. Janey scooped up Purry-Motor and slammed into the kitchen.

Elinor was slicing bread on the cutting board.

"What in the world is the matter?" she asked.

"Amy said Norma can't stay for supper and Norma went home mad." Janey grumbled. "I wouldn't blame her if she never spoke to me again."

Elinor frowned at Amy's disappearing back as she headed for the stairs. "It's not like Amy to be mean," she said. "So she must have a good reason. I'm sure she'll tell us in her own good time. Set the table for four, then, Jane. The boys won't be home for supper tonight."

Janey got the bluebell plates out of the kitchen cabinet and shuffled them around the kitchen table.

John Phair came in the front door, hung up his coat, and breezed into the kitchen. He kissed his wife right on the lips — Janey couldn't get over that — and pinched Janey's cheek. Then he said, "Where's the rest of my squad?"

"Amy's upstairs and the boys are working," explained Elinor. "You can call your sister now, Jane."

Janey yelled up the stairs and Amy came straight down. Her cheeks were pink and she looked excited about something.

But whatever news Amy was bursting with, she managed to hold it in until her father had finished eating. When he was contentedly drinking his tea she said, "I have something to discuss with you, Father." Then she looked from her father to her stepmother to her sister. "With all of you," she amended.

John Phair set his teacup down and gave her his full attention. "We're listening," he said.

Amy took a deep breath and plunged in. "Winnie Plum is going to Kingston Normal School and I want to go with her."

"Kingston!" Janey couldn't have been more surprised if her sister had said she wanted to go to school on the moon.

"*Kingston!*" her father roared. "Who in blazes put that crackpot idea into your head?"

"Well . . . Winnie and I sent our applications in at the end of June and we've both been accepted."

Amy drew a letter out of her skirt pocket and handed it hesitantly to her father.

He read it without a word and handed it to Elinor. She read it and passed it on to Janey.

The letter was from Kingston Normal School and it said that Miss Amy Phair's application had been accepted for the Fall Semester.

"I'm waiting for an explanation," her father said.

So Amy took another deep breath. "Winnie's aunt . . . Mrs. Plum's sister . . . lives in Kingston and she has an extra bedroom with a double bed and she says I can share it with Winnie and it will only cost five dollars a week for room and board. And . . . "

"Oh, boy!" squealed Janey. "I'll get my own bedroom!"

"Shush!" her father said. Then he turned to Amy. "It's out of the question. I can't afford it. I'm not a banker like Mr. Plum, you know."

"But you didn't let me finish, Father," Amy said. "It won't cost more money. Winnie's aunt will let me earn my room and board by doing the cleaning and baking. You know I'm good at that. And Winnie says she'll help me."

There was silence around the table.

Then Elinor spoke quietly, "It seems to me that Amy has thought this through very carefully. And if she needs a little extra money we can always make her a loan."

"And you can have my seven dollars that I got for my birthday, Amy," Janey said. "I don't even need it." And if Daddy objects, she thought, I'll remind him that we women are equals now that we've got the vote.

She had her mouth all set to argue when her father suddenly threw up his hands in surrender. "I give up! I'm no match for the lot of you. You're a bunch of conspirators if you ask me." He left the table and went into the sitting room, and they heard him chuckling to himself as he cracked open his evening paper.

Chapter 30

New Beginnings

Early in the morning, the day after Labour Day, Winnie Plum and Amy Phair were settled in the back seat of Mr. Plum's Hupmobile. Their leather grips were fastened to the running board by a folding metal fence stretched across like a gate.

The whole Phair family was gathered on the sidewalk to say goodbye. Janey was leaning in the car window. "Will you write to me as soon as you get there, Amy?"

She had mixed feeling about her sister leaving. Oh, it would be swell to have the bed all to herself, but . . . "I'm going to miss you, Amy," she said, blinking hard.

"I'll miss you, too, Janey." Amy reached out and pulled one of Janey's chestnut curls. "Promise me you'll work hard this year."

"I will," Janey promised. She kissed her sister

on the cheek. Then her father moved her aside.

Leaning his elbows on the car door he looked at Amy wistfully. "Well, Vinny . . . " he said.

"Well, Father . . . Dad . . . "

"Be a good girl. But you've always been that. You two girls take care of each other."

"We will, Mr. Phair. Don't worry," Winnie assured him. "My Auntie Em is very strict. She'll send us straight home if we make a speck of trouble." They laughed.

Then Mr. Plum said, "Well, we'd best be on our way. We've got a long trip ahead of us." He started the motor and revved up the engine.

Suddenly Elinor pushed past everybody. Reaching through the car window she drew Amy into her arms. Over Elinor's shoulder, Janey saw Amy's eyes glistening. Then she heard her say, "Thanks for everything . . . Elinor." It was the first time Amy had ever called their stepmother by name.

They stood on the sidewalk in front of the purple house, waving and calling goodbye, until the Hupmobile disappeared around the corner. Then Mike and Pat and their father went inside for breakfast.

Janey and Elinor stayed on the sidewalk, their arms around each other, gazing down the empty street. Then they looked at each other and their eyes were bright with tears.

"Thank you, Mother," Janey said.

"Oh, Jane . . . " Elinor hugged Janey so hard it hurt. "No one has ever called me that before."

And Janey answered, "I've never said it to anyone before."

Bernice Thurman Hunter was a storyteller from an early age, but it was not until her children were grown that she began to get her work published. Now she is one of Canada's favourite writers of historical fiction, with a dozen books to her credit, including the *Booky* and *Margaret* trilogies, *Lamplighter*, *The Railroader*, *The Firefighter*, *Hawk and Stretch* and, of course, *Amy's Promise*.

One of Bernice's greatest strengths as a writer is her ability to bring her childhood memories to vivid life for readers of all ages. She has received many awards, including the Vicky Metcalf award for her contribution to Canadian children's literature. *Amy's Promise*, the first book about the Phair family, was the winner of the 1997 Red Cedar Award.

Bernice lives in Toronto, Ontario.